PARADISE ROAD

Drue Heinz Literature Prize 2007

Paradise Road

KIRK NESSET

University of Pittsburgh Press

Published by the University of Pittsburgh Press, Pittsburgh, PA 15260

Manufactured in the United States of America

Printed on acid-free paper

10 9 8 7 6 5 4 3 2 1

Library of Congress Cataloging-in-Publication Data

Nesset, Kirk.
    Paradise road / Kirk Nesset.
        p.   cm.
    "Drue Heinz Literature Prize 2007."
    ISBN-13: 978-0-8229-4315-0 (alk. paper)
    ISBN-10: 0-8229-4315-8 (alk. paper)
    I. Title.
    PS3614.E499P37 2007
    813'.6—dc22   2007025336

for Barry Spacks

CONTENTS

The Prince of Perch Fishing   1

Hers   34

Paradise Road   39

Still Life with Candles and Spanish Guitar   57

Salvage   63

Be with Somebody   76

Poet and Philosopher   89

The Dead Know Too Much   98

Record Shop Girl   104

Good Is All You Know How to Be   116

The Painter's Wife   125

Somebody Decent   127

Acknowledgments   *139*

PARADISE ROAD

The Prince of Perch Fishing

Widow Fudge was widowed young. Her husband, a smiling sandy-haired broker, met his end on Highway 116, east of Jenner, near the mouth of the river, thanks to thick fog and a seven-ton ready-mix truck. The husband she had before that died in Montana, off up in the hills, an accident of some kind while elk hunting. She'd lived on her own these nine years or so as far we knew. She had a degree in history from the state university and a wicked way with retorts. She was forty-eight but looked younger. She had that sparkle and spark everyone likes and looks for in people. She kicked ass in chess; she was trim and fit from riding her bicycle. If anybody had a chance with her it should've been Reverend Bob, prince of perch fishing, truly a character, an actor in community theater, not even remotely tormented, so wry and dry in his hilarious way.

We met Wednesdays at midday to fish, Bob and Casper and Leo and me and a few other oddballs, on a dock on the north end of the bay alongside the less lovely marina. We sat on folding stools and on ice chests and buckets, watching our bobbers and gossiping, discussing kids and grandkids and berating the government, lamenting above all the price of gas. We drank coffee or pop and hauled a fish up now and then and nobody kept anything, unless whatever it was was too big or too stuck to pass up. If you watched, around one or one-thirty, you'd see Widow Fudge curving down the hill on her bicycle. Down the steep grade she'd fly, past the saltwater taffy and kite shop and the quick-fill and Bodega Gallery, which offered tourist-grade art—fishing boats floating shrouded in fog, sea boulders battered by surf, gulls standing on pilings with foggy sunsets beyond. She'd hitch her bike to the fence in the dirt lot and head down the slatted ramp, carrying a bag she'd pull from her wicker bike basket, a bag of zucchini muffins or carrot bread or cookies usually, nothing too sinful, fixing the pins in her hair as she went. Even the dullest and deadest among us would brighten, hearing her step.

Well, what have you learned? she'd ask, addressing us all.

Not one single thing, Lady Fudge, Reverend Bob would respond, shaking his head for the rest of us. It's a whimsical world, he'd say—or something similar, equally philosophical. And add: What's in the bag? Whiskey?

She'd scowl and ask who caught what. If the action was slow she'd ask what was the matter; clearly, she'd say, what we were lacking was drive. All the while she stepped along between us—Bob and Casper and Hammond and Leo B. Jensen and me and whoever (flannel shirts, windbreakers, Dacron vests)—and over and around the obstacle course of tackle boxes, bait bags, creels, and coolers. She didn't exactly tower over us, either. She stood maybe four-foot-ten in her high-soled sneakers and jeans, hair piled in a windblown blond bun on her head. She'd accept a diet Sprite or a cup of black coffee from somebody's thermos and tell us how worthless we were but she loved us anyway. Then she'd pull a hand line out of her purse—she didn't own a rod or reel—and get a bit of bait and toss her baited hook off the dock with her bobber.

Somebody needs to get lucky here, she'd say. Guess it'll have to be me.

What made things different today was the fact that I'd spent two nights at her house in Shell Beach. Tonight would make three. I'd had a termite tent thrown over my own place in Camp Meeker, and, well, Widow Fudge had a guest room, and insisted I stay, rather than go to the motel as planned. My buddies knew already, amazingly. Casper suspected and he'd opened his mouth, I suppose. But I'd had a sweet visit. We chopped onions and chilies and cilantro for salsa, the widow and I, and watched the news on the tube and did crosswords, there in her cedar cottage overlooking the sea.

What a sad pack of baboons, the widow said, settling down. Are we out of bait?

Reverend Bob scooted his bag her way, and the cutting board and knife. The sun shone bright, rare for July. Just a hint of fog. Casper asked Hammond how the work was coming. Hammond was painting his house on the inside in something called Amaranth Glow. Just now they were waiting for more. More amaranth paint. Casper asked Hammond, bloated red-bearded Hammond, how he liked his Viagra.

That's idiotic, the widow said.

Why? Hammond asked.

It's like putting a flagpole on a condemned building, she said.

We had an outgoing tide today, which meant less fish. Bob had caught one puny perch. The water'd dropped down the sea wall, fifty yards out. Barnacles and mussels gleamed on the creosoted lower slats and on posts and pilings. Even starfish were exposed. Pale purple, pink, and pale green.

So what do you know? the widow asked Bob.

Beer and chain saws, he said.

In that order?

Whichever.

He sat hunched over his knees on his yellow bucket, wilted somewhat, his vest off and top button unbuttoned. He was balding in front, with a philosopher's forehead; his tidy gray ponytail lapped at his collar. Casper and Hammond sat to the right, and Leo beyond them, applying fresh bait, a section of anchovy, peering though his trifocals, grinning. He had his hearing aid cranked, evidently.

What made things different today was the fact that I'd landed in her bedroom after my night in the guest room. There'd been beer and salsa and chips and then snapper and salad and wine, the sun sinking into the Pacific, and more wine, then brandy. And then maybe four blurry words of a crossword and a fuzzy tussle on the living room floor, then bed. We were both embarrassed, I guess. She wouldn't even look at me now. Add to this the fact that she and Reverend Bob were involved in a way; he'd called her house twice while I was there.

The thing was, Bob was my friend. We'd hung at the bar at Negri's for years, hadn't missed an Occidental Firemen's Dance in a decade. He was my partner in crime, as they say. Overbearing, yes, and self-serving at times, but a friend I could count on. Before he retired he did construction, small-scale contracting; for a while I was part of his electrical team. He helped me put my retaining wall in, no easy job, and came to my aid when my wife Kay wigged out on Zoloft and decided, after thirty-three years of marriage, she'd had enough. He sat and listened, and listened and sat, and carted my pistol off finally, and poured the pain pills and shitty gin I had down the sink. He started Fishing Day at the Bay after that, looking for ways maybe to occupy me. To get me and us out to shoot the shit and soak up the fog and salt breeze.

A salmon boat boiled up the channel, dirty white with blue trim. It cut its engine and eased into the marina trailed by gulls. Its wake made our dock rock. I felt elated and faithless at once. I felt electrified crown to toenail. I felt like a cad. A kid came down the ramp, baggy pants, ball cap. Bob looked at Hammond and Hammond got up, groaning, and intercepted the kid. This was a private dock, but Bob knew Monty the owner. Bob had invited Leo and Hammond and most of the others. Casper was recruited by me. He lived down the hill from me, on the same road. He was the only friend I had besides Bob.

In the marina, off left, salmon boats were unloading. The bay was almost unnervingly calm. Bob looked unwell. The widow unzipped the zipper at her collar, brushed a wisp of hair from her eyes. She had her lavender fleece on, beyond extra-small, something designed for a child, it looked like. The color was there in her cheeks, the faint raspberry swirl in gourmet ice cream. I felt her in every cell of my body. I felt her heat, her heartbeat. I could taste her violet-almond perfume. I had to keep looking away. I'd rehearsed something to say but the time never came. I was doing all I could to not look like I felt, to not melt through the cracks in the dock. You were gone before I woke up, I might've said. Or: what about Bob? I wasn't sure at first in the haze if I hadn't dreamt what we did.

A gull lit on the rail, cocking its head at my bait bag. Another boat churned in past the sea wall. We sat watching our bobbers. Leo slept, head slumped on his chest. Bob looked at me and kept looking. I looked back at him.

Did you or didn't you? his look seemed to say.

My look answered his.

Casper got up off his collapsible stool, grunting. He stood facing Bob momentarily, then the widow.

Marion, where's my cookie, he said. He eyed the bakery bag at her feet.

You haven't earned yours, she said.

What about Leo B. Jensen? Leo asked in his rasp, waking up.

Catch a fish first.

He sputtered something else I couldn't make out. And then coughed. He'd smoked cigars fifty years of his life. No cancer, but his voice box was shot.

The widow's bobber jumped, though she hadn't been here ten minutes. She jerked her hand line.

Guess it'll have to be me that gets lucky, she said.

Casper squinched up his face—something like a grimace.

Chuck's the one's got the luck, he said, looking at me.

The widow's bobber grew still. Bob reeled in a couple of clicks, staring straight ahead. And then sighed.

Casper, you're about as subtle as a salami, he said.

I drove north up the coast to the mouth of the river and followed the river inland to Guerneville, wanting to buy groceries, a blackberry pie perhaps and a red rose for the widow, and putty and bolts to fix her bathroom door. It took awhile; the winding two-lane was slow, and closer to town it was stop and go, stop and go, past the dusty redwoods and firs and dolled-up resorts, the wooden marquees and strings of colored lanterns, with here and there green glimpses of river. It was midweek, so no festival to blame, no jazz on the beach, no Stump Town dementia, no rodeo, no winery weekend mob, no convocation of gay bikers, black leather and biceps and painted-on tank tops. It was July on the river, simple as that. Guerneville was packed, crammed to the gills with vacationers up from San Fran or the east or south bay or out from Santa Rosa for the day to ditch the heat. It took me all but an hour to shop and check out at Safeway, to buy the pie and avocado and greens, the gallon jugs of drinking water, the pork loin and veal and can of cashews she liked, and for the ride home in the pickup, the chilled six-pack of Mickey's. I slipped into Etter's for hardware and heading west finally, cracked a bottle. At Monte Rio I crossed the bridge, hung a right, passed Bartlett's and The Pink and wound south on 12, the alternate route, the long way, the back way, not wanting to get there too soon.

Let the widow wonder where I went, I guess I was thinking.

Or maybe not thinking: just doing what I did when I fell into things, which wasn't often. I wondered what in the hell I'd done, what I was doing. It all felt like bewitchment and magic. I felt giddy and weird. And glad overall, yes, about the spell I was under, suspect as I might that the spell would dissolve, Bob or no Bob.

My town was less than a pause on the alternate route, just a carved redwood sign, *Welcome to Camp Meeker!,* and a tiny store and P.O. at the base of several steep hills, with narrow roads winding through the shadow-drenched canyons and up out of the dark. Occupying the main drag was the camp, sixty-three acres of wooded land and mosquitoes with a creek flowing through, reserved years in advance by organizations of Christians, student musicians, Republicans, psychics and spiritual healers, romance writers, student actors and Boy Scouts and Cubs and Campfires and Brownies. Dykes on Bikes, a lesbian bike gang from the City, rolled in for ten days several summers ago, but one of the bikers beat up a heckler, reconfigured his face for him and broke his knee and elbow; since then they've convened in spots a bit more remote.

My house on Tower Hill was still shrouded in its red and white covering. A great poison circus, it seemed, cheerfully deadly, if lopsided, drained. I stopped and gaped, window rolled down. They'd had to blast the place twice, my termite situation was grave. The tent would come off tomorrow; I could bring my plants and fish tank back Friday. I edged up to my mailbox and got my mail and curved down the hill again. In the deep dim at the bottom, on the redwood-frond floor of the canyon, Casper was waiting. He'd seen me pass going up; he stood in the road now in front of his house.

What? I said, rolling my window down.

Slow up, he told me. Critters got the right of way here.

Says who?

Some fuck squashed a king snake across the way yesterday. He pointed. Stain's right there, if you care to see.

He still had the fishing duds on, the pumpkin-orange windbreaker and heavy khaki overalls, the green neon knit cap. His face was shaded with patches of black and gray stubble. Around us the cicadas were loud, scratching their electrical buzz.

I wasn't up here, I said. I didn't hit any snake.

You moved out or what?

Sure.

I told Bob you two should arm-wrestle for her.

A pair of jays swooped across in a blur of blue and lit above us somewhere, rasping and squawking.

Aren't you hot dressed like that? I asked.

How?

It's ninety degrees out.

7

I just got here. You left early, remember? You should've seen the run of jack smelt we got. Big one pulled Bob's pole right in. Took us twenty minutes to fish it out.

Liar, I said.

The fish was still on it. Big fucker. Close to twelve pounds.

A truck came up behind us and braked. The jays scattered; I pulled my pickup to the shoulder. The truck lurched around and ahead.

Dick ass, Casper hissed in the dust.

I pushed the clutch in and said, See you later, I guess.

He glanced into the cab. The pie lay in its tin on my passenger seat. A plant sat beside it, a houseplant, deep green swirled with white, in a black plastic pot. A rose in the end had seemed a bit too romantic. A replacement, this, for the one the widow drowned in her den.

You see Bob?

When? I said.

Now. He come down just before you went up.

I have to go.

She ought to decide, you ask me.

He took a step back. And pulled his cap off, and did something like mop his brow with it. And said: Don't squish any snakes as you go, Romeo. He had more to say, I could see, but by then I was gone, heading out into the sun.

———

She grew up on a ranch in Wyoming, miles away from anything, and had lived in Laredo, El Paso, Great Falls, and Fort Wayne. She moved here from L.A. with husband the second, the broker Fuchmueller, and for years rode back and forth to the university to study, a forty-five or fifty minute drive if it wasn't too foggy. Broker Fudge had retired by this point but retained an office in Sebastopol to do the consulting and what have you. I met him at a wedding before the collision that killed him, and met her too, though he stuck out most. Another extravagant import, I think I remember myself thinking. Regal but thoughtful, good posture, poised, a little lined but not balding, with that air of charity that comes of not having to worry about money.

So she got her degree and started an internet thing at home for her master's, above all it seemed to keep busy, busy as she was buying and selling rental properties, coastal and inland, haranguing her property managers, e-mailing, shopping, doing her sit-ups and leg lifts and aiding in charities, of which there were many. Wednesday afternoons she fished, like I said. It was a serious pedal from her place to the bay, seven miles up switchback and down on roads with no shoulder, or barely any. Still, down the hill she'd come on her bike—she didn't drive, never had—with a bag in her basket and fishing line wrapped on a stick. I didn't know what to think those first weeks. She stupefied me. She was exotic, outspoken, good-looking, rich. She was tiny but didn't take any shit, from us or anybody. She'd stamp the dock in her way and say, What a shit bird you are, or, You're cute but you're worthless, and dismiss the lot of us, sad pack of apes that we were.

Why did she keep coming back, pedaling through fog and chill wind?

At first I thought we were just another of her charities, Bob and Casper and me and the cronies, abuse us as she did with her peremptory statements and withholding of cookies. Then I thought she'd come to see Bob. Then I *knew* she'd come to see Bob, who carted her back and forth for a while to Sonoma State in Cotati, not far from where he worked remodeling condos. But now I didn't know what I knew. Except that Bob had a wife, a decent sweet woman he'd been with since high school. And that he was my friend, pissed as I was about this thing or that thing he had done or said. He could be a monumental ass at times, actually. Even still, I was entwined in this now. I'd entered it willfully, consciously, selfishly. And not, as my conscience kept saying, to spare Karen, unstinting Karen, his wife.

So in my fumbling way I pursued her, I guess. I mean Widow Fudge. She rode with me back from the dock those times it got nasty rainy. We went to The Tides and had clam chowder and coffee while waves slapped the pier underneath, her soaked bike in my pickup. We went to the Oyster Tavern in Marshall in May, way out of her way, and talked about Kay my ex and my son in Marin, popped again for selling illegal goods, ecstasy mainly and these pills they give kids to make them less twitchy. The widow didn't let on much as far as her own life was concerned. She wouldn't say a single thing about Bob. She liked keeping things light and abrupt, crass or uncouth or otherwise. It was like we were actors in some kind of backwater comedy.

Why history? I asked her that day, at the tavern in Marshall.

Because I'm so bad with dates, she replied.

I'll be your date, I said, momentarily witty, like Bob.

She said, Like hell you will be. What'll you do to impress me?

I didn't have a quick answer for that. I might have shrugged, or took a slug off my beer bottle.

Well? she said.

I'll wash all that salt spray off your windows. Somebody's got to.

She looked at me, both pleased, I think, and put off.

What else?

I'll tie you up in your attic. For a week. You'll be stuck there.

She raised her eyebrows.

And then what'll you do?

The waiter came and carried the oyster shells away on their plates and the carnage of fish bones—we'd ordered dinner. I'd painted myself into a kind of corner, talking this way. We'd had tequila, I'd gotten bold. I was afraid to imagine what I might say.

I'll get down in front of you, I think I said.

And then what? What'll you do?

Worship you.

She took this in even as she brushed it away, laughing. She leaned on her elbows, reigning over the mess on the table of limes and salt and little tubs of Tabasco.

And then I'll get bored, she said. And then we won't date. And then you'll be history.

On up over the hill to Occidental I drove, past the Union Hotel and Negri's and Tim's, past the town hall and bank with their reconstructed frontier facades, on out of town past the goat farm and up Coleman Valley to my cousin Fred's property and his sheet-metal shed. Fred was in Saskatchewan fishing, gone for six weeks; had his cats not made my eyes itch I'd have house-sat for him. I undid the padlock on the sheet-metal door, slid the bolt across, and started hauling water jugs in, plastic gallons of Safeway drinking water. I had twenty or more in the bed of my pickup. But before I got half of them in I heard an engine. I fairly leapt out of the shed again. And around the dirt bend came Reverend Bob, bumping along in his Ranger.

Figured you might be heading here, he said, pulling up. The dust settled around him, around us. His tall forehead shone, from the heat perhaps, or concern. He looked like he'd swallowed a rotten squirrel. Need a hand? he said.

You followed me here?

He got out and grabbed a pair of jugs and walked in behind me.

You passed me at the Arco. I thought you saw me wave.

Stepping into the smell in that shed was like stepping into a wall. Beyond the boxes of dishes and cookware, the clothes and towels and blankets and sheets, beyond my fish tank and bulbous bubble-eyed goldfish, thirty fat pot plants stood in tight rows, a blurry olive green woods. It was hotter than shit in that shed; the smell was layered and thick, obnoxious, intense.

Kids are looking good, Bob said.

Mostly, I said.

Actually they'd been in the dark three days now and looked a bit stunned. They were nodding a little, missing the grow lights. We gave each plant a drink, a half gallon roughly, more for the tallest and woolliest. I didn't say anything and neither did Bob. He wore his Raiders tank top, gold on black, and jean shorts, rubber thongs.

He stood six-two or taller, with a hint of a gut on him and a beer drinker's nose. He was a redneck turned hippie turned hick renaissance man, a connoisseur of slow living and a self-professed slouch, a fan of Joseph Conrad and Dickens, fond of young women but not fool enough to think he could bag what he couldn't. We called him Reverend, but he wasn't one and never had been. He'd been a vicar or deacon in a play at some point and somebody started calling him that: Reverend Bob. He did tend now and then to pronounce. To stand before an invisible crowd and expound, if not preach.

He glanced at my boxes up front. They were barricading the door, sort of.

They say termite gas won't hurt your dishes.

So they say.

Or your clothes. It dissolves.

I don't trust it, I said.

Thinking: Nothing comes and goes with no trace. It might be true, what they said about Vikane, this gas that was ending even now the last of those last termite lives. But it didn't sound right to me, or possible. In this world there are consequences for everything. The termite squad knew a lot, but not all. The same went for Bob.

We emptied the last of the jugs and stood staring a moment. I sprinkled a pinch of food flakes in the fish tank. The fish moved toward the top leisurely, mouths working, eyes bugged, trailing their billowing fins.

Do what you need to do, Bob told me.

I have been.

I can see that, he said.

I'd had no choice but to transport the plants here, since I only owned a quarter-acre, neighbors on all sides. Bob's house of course was off-limits. Karen, his wife, didn't know and wouldn't approve; they had too much to lose, and there were kids and grandkids around. It was either let my house, which I was planning to sell, go to hell, or forsake our harvest. Each of these plants would yield ten grand or more, come October. Two hundred forty thousand for me, sixty for Bob. He taught me all this three seasons ago. The Art of Cultivating for Profit, along with the Art of Not Getting Caught. I bore the great share of danger, and watered and clipped. He came each week to inspect. He made the connection too, finally, met with the buyer, or buyers, and knew all the cops in town, and a judge.

He stood now facing a belly-high plant. Wielding my pruning tool, he severed a lower branch, then pinched some sticky tops, those skunky red-purple buds. He snapped the tips off another, sighing, and stuffed the tips in a Ziploc. He bent toward one more, inspecting. The wind rose outside. It shook the leaves on the bay trees and tan oaks and blew dust in the door. A little rude, this, on Bob's part, if not quite imprudent—above and beyond the call it seemed of strategic pruning. He folded the Ziploc and stuck it in his shorts pocket. He smoked the stuff, unlike yours truly, averse as I was to burning up profits, and not fond of the drug. It made me feel more self-conscious and inward than I already was.

Worse, his proprietorial air lately upset me. These trees were mine, basically. I tended them, coaxed them with heat and light and nutrients, was watchful with water. I talked to them. I called them courageous, I said they were pretty. I dreamt about their safety, and mine. I felt something like physical pain seeing them manhandled thus. Indeed they were my kids. By this point I'd read all the books, had gone to the web sites, I'd talked to growers online. I knew more about the art now than Bob did. And I could tell he was less than pleased about this.

Aren't I the one who's supposed to be mad? he asked me.

He set my pruning shears down, sniffed his fingers. We looked at each other. For a moment I thought he might hit me. He tugged at his ponytail, looked away, and said, Isn't that how it goes?

How does what go?

Jesus.

She's not somebody you'd hang onto anyway.

Chuck, you're an odd piece of shit. You know that? You might at least give a guy a chance.

We stepped into the hot breeze and dust. I jerked the bolt across and snapped the padlock.

To do what? I asked.

To tell you you're a son of a bitch.

I pulled on the padlock to make sure it held. I'm sorry, I said.

Just ask her how her first husband bit it. That ought to do it.

Right.

I mean it. Have her show you her guns.

Tomorrow at midnight I'd have the shell back on my truck and would cart the kids home. Two per garbage bag, each wedged gently in, each tipped on its side. It would be faster and safer with Bob there to help me. But I could see now I'd be working alone. Which was what I wanted. And had been wanting, admit it or not, for God knows how long.

———————

Later I carried the groceries in, called out to her, waited. I stood on the deck in the wind, then stepped inside and called out again. I checked her room and the den and guest room and gym and the room she had her desk in and books and computer. She wasn't home. The lights were on and her bike had arrived; it stood askew on its kickstand on the walkway outside. Her newspaper crossword lay half-done on the dining table. And here was her pen, which erased, and beside it the wineglass emptied of wine. It was maybe an hour past sunset. The sky out her windows was pink, more like flamingo and orange by the ocean horizon. I was staggered again by the view. The sea and sky and whitecaps, the bent cypresses gripping the cliff, the boom and thunder of surf—it all made my heart hurt somehow.

Outside past the deck I followed the curving path through clumps of ice plant and spike grass and the mini–sand dunes to the cliff and looked over the edge for her. I looked both ways up the beach, wind stinging my face. I saw cords of bull kelp with their tasseled heads and shiny mounds of tangled sea grass and wet driftwood. I saw foam at the surf line, I saw a battered bleach bottle. But no widow. And no footprints, either. Nobody'd been down there at all. I glanced at her house, its cedar siding gray from the weather, light twinkling out from the skylights and windows. If she was around I couldn't see her. A wave hit the cliff so hard I felt the shock where I stood. The heavy cypress beside me, misshapen and hunched in the way of cypresses here, grew not so much upward as back, stuck in the shape the wind blew it in.

I opened the garage as daylight faded and wheeled the bicycle up, propped it there among the dead fitness machines and boxes of pictures and knickknacks and papers and books. I wiped the mist off the thing and oiled it with some oil I found—the gears and sprocket were suffering, the chain corroded—and I tightened the brakes. It was a child's bike, blue and hot pink, made for a little girl, a mountain-street hybrid with a blue and pink basket. It had a little horn, even, with the rubber bulb that you squeeze. All it lacked were tassels, the plastic streamers on the handlebar grips. Inside I got a beer from the fridge, one of hers—my Mickeys' were warm—and then thought what the fuck and poured a few shots of her gin in a glass for myself and sipped it, then swallowed it down.

The plan was that come winter I'd be buying the house I had my eye on in Jenner. A sweet, wide, open-beam place on the side of the mountain, views of the ocean and river mouth and wrecked dock and sandbar and bellowing sea lions. The plan was, even before we ever got serious, that we'd move in together out there, in Jenner, the widow and I, since it was bigger and closer to town, to cafes and shopping, but that she would keep this place on the cliff to, as she put it, escape when she had to from me. It was a kind of joke we had. A silly romantic plan, both a joke and not a joke. Less so for me, I think, than for her.

I called her name out again, and listened. I didn't hear a thing but the wind, which rattled the windows. In her gym room I studied the controls on the exercycle and stairwalker and treadmill, beer in hand; then I washed up in her bathroom, the big one with its two sinks inset in marble and filigreed mirrors and whirlpool bath. I eyeballed the mail on the bar in the kitchen and tried to listen to the messages on her message machine, but they'd been erased.

In order to do it right, of course, I'd need a few more harvests.

Three would do it, I thought. My paltry retirement and social security wouldn't cut it, even with the cash I'd get from the house in Camp Meeker and my bag of gold coins, which sat in a box in the vault at the bank. No, if we moved in together she'd meet my kids, she'd have to. I didn't imagine she'd like them one bit. She wasn't amused at the thought, I could tell, of my son and his mishap and six months to go still in jail in Mill Valley. She hailed from Wyoming, the high plains, not here. Not California, land of love and burnt bras and drugs, of just saying no to those who say no, of bee pollen and wheat grass and nutritional plankton.

Her guns stood in a rack in the hall closet, behind the raincoats and woolens, things hanging on hangers. I clicked the light on and, parting the clothing, knelt down to look. A twenty-two, chipped up somewhat, not new. A thirty-ought-six, newer, enough to knock a full-grown caribou down. And a shotgun; and an antique pistol of sorts, a relic, something Buffalo Bill might have used in his wild west show. I pulled the shotgun off and examined the thing. It was loaded, I noticed. All her guns needed oil. They cried out to be cleaned, this one especially. I unhooked the safety.

Where've you been? she said.

She'd snuck in behind me. I stood up too fast and banged my skull on the overhang. I didn't drop the shotgun, luckily.

Here, I told her. I snapped the safety back and tucked the shotgun in. Where were you? I asked, following her out of the closet. I touched my scalp where it hit.

That's what you get, she said, for getting into my stuff.

I like your stuff.

She noticed the pie on the counter, the plant in its pot and translucent coaster.

What a dear man you are, she exclaimed.

Dearer than Bob? I wanted to say. She had on a light pink sweat suit and tiny white socks, her hair swept up in a tail. My heart about broke, seeing her.

There's lots more dear where that dearness came from, I said instead.

I'll bet.

She pulled a pair of wineglasses out and the jug of wine from the fridge. The wind roared outside. Something clunked on the porch.

I'll be heading home tomorrow, I told her.

What's the hurry? she asked. She tipped the wine jug over the glasses, saw the beer in my hand, and filled just the one. White zinfandel from a screw-cap bottle. She filled it to the top, or all but.

You don't want me to go?

Would you stay if I did?

I might.

She raised her drink and we clinked. Her wineglass, my bottle.

I like you, she said. But you're sneaky.

I am not sneaky, I told her, and she said, Oh yes you are, and then tugged my head down and kissed me. And said, I like you sneaky, and let me go, then held me again.

At least I'm not bored, she said.

Then she led me off down the hall to the bed. Two days more would go by before I'd get myself home, though I would move the kids back the next night and feed and console them and settle them in. And for the life of me I couldn't begin to decide who this Widow Fudge was, after five days and five nights in her house and more talk and jokes and kissing and bathing. She was a tiny wiry thing, unyielding as metal but not without softness, especially now with the wind in a rage and the sea screaming, her yellow pillows perfumed. Her guard dropped and something new and different, something deeper, shone through. I'd known her for ages it seemed, but in some other language, or landscape, or realm. In some ocean, or primordial hothouse, some bountiful celestial cell.

––––––––

I was glad to be home, empty and weird as I felt at first. I got unpacked box by box and tended my plants and tried to call Bob, but Bob wouldn't respond. I put fresh stain on my deck and front steps and touched up my trim. I scrubbed the place good and washed the windows and raked and had more gravel delivered to make the drive pretty. The poison had made a clean sweep; not a creature was stirring, neither termite nor mouse. I put my house on the market, according to plan. The appraiser came and appraised. My place was worth more than I thought; the gay influx persisted and gay meant money and money meant higher prices for property. My attic was safe, I should say, from the prying eyes of appraisers. It was sealed tight. No light escaped. My kids had an air filter, too, potent if quiet; it sucked the smell almost completely away. The new owners would have to discover the entrance, the portal, the camouflaged door and secret stairwell Bob helped me build.

In the meantime, I went to the widow's to eat or she came to mine. Now and then I'd stay over, but not often. We'd cooled some after my marathon visit, with backing off on both our parts, but I felt we were with it, I felt the richness increase. She was impressed by the fact that I had in fact done it. That I'd got the ball rolling toward Jenner, toward shedding this place with its echo of Kay, my ex, just like I said I would. The widow saw now I wasn't all talk and no action. I was trading my dank deep woods for the coast. Granted, 1.5 million was slightly out of my price range for houses. But I could see my way now, and she could see I would show her.

I didn't drive out to the dock to fish, and neither did Bob.

People came to look at my house. Then I had an offer, and another offer, all of this in ten days or less, and I accepted, and my house was sold. Sale contingent, that is, on seller remaining in said house on said property on Tower Hill in Camp Meeker until late October; seller would be purchasing upgrade and unloading dope.

On the verge of September, this was. Then we were into September, the days warm and fine, and Bob still didn't fish, nor did I, though Widow Fudge did. None of this fazed her, oddly. The Bob problem came up a few times and she told me she and Bob were a passing thing. She said he was worthless, though funny. She said Bob was sneakier even and more shady than I was, as far as that went. And why do that to his wife? She told me he told her his marriage was more or less over; she told me she told him she'd heard that one before.

I called my son Ted every few days as usual. I went to visit him twice; he sat behind glass at the compound, a very clean jail, in Marin. He swore to God he'd be good now, he would completely behave. I felt sorry for him, and sorry I couldn't share tales of my kids with my kid for fear of making his delinquency worse, when to be truthful he'd worsened mine. I called Bob again and again and finally gave up. He wouldn't answer his cell phone and must have instructed Karen not to pick up at home. I didn't want a boss anymore; but I didn't want things not to be right with us, either.

So when Casper came over I was willing to bend but was pissed also. I hadn't done anything that awful to Bob. I didn't steal his squeeze. She'd stolen me. I hadn't done any nasty outrageous thing or acted in spite. I wasn't a son of a bitch or a dirty shit or a bastard. He'd been wanting to hate me and just needed a reason, a bona fide cause. So I was sitting making lists in my kitchen when he knocked. Casper, that is. Knocked his unmistakable knock, both brash and unsure, as if he couldn't say if this was the house but he'd go ahead and whack the door anyway. It was like nine, ten o'clock at night. He came in and sat down and I got him a gin. He liked his with fruit juice, not tonic.

He said he saw the sold sign out front, good job. How long would I be here for? Six or eight weeks, I said. Depending. Long as the gay boys don't buy it and make it buttfuck central, he said, I don't mind. I laughed and said, Don't be an ass. He looked bedraggled as usual, rumpled and pinched, jeans and boots and dirty red cotton hood, not complacent but not willing either to squawk about the place he was in. He worked for the quote-unquote Sewer Authority, had been there twenty-four years; six to go before he retired. A seriously weird man, Casper. I liked him, and couldn't say why. He lacked tact but endeared. He had integrity, bizarre as it was.

Fishing tomorrow? he asked, since this was Tuesday.

I'm kind of busy, I said.

Bob's gonna be there, he told me. We hope.

So?

It's been like a month. He was sicker than shit. Hammond and me went over to his place Friday. We told him he had to come down. Wednesday. Or else. We ain't catching shit now.

Try different bait.

He took a big slug off his gin and Cranapple.

Try tube worms, I said.

They hate my jokes, he said, spitting an ice cube back in his glass. Widow's gonna brain me if you don't do something.

I got the phone off the counter and gave it to him. And said, All right fine, call him, we'll talk and this'll all be okay.

Casper did as I said, pushed Bob's numbers in as dictated. Then listened, looking like the phone might melt in his hand. I had half a heat on by this point and felt fairly bold, basking in the glow of my house being sold and newly pissed off at Bob. Pissed at Bob, that is, for staying pissed off at me. Pissed at him taking any chick he wanted and telling me about it in his woebegone way, as if the chicks weren't his fault but just happened, like traps set to confuse. I was pissed at Bob for being Bob, basically. For groping my plants; for sneaking out on his wife the way mine had snuck out on me.

Bob didn't pick up, but his voice mail came on.

Bob, it's me, Casper, Casper said, and stopped, at a loss.

And Chuck, I said, leaning over.

We're fishing tomorrow. With you, without you.

We need you, I said.

Hammond's bringing a case just so you show. Case of Sam Adams, or Pete's.

I'm bringing whiskey.

Chuck's bringing whiskey.

Damn skippy.

Be there or be queer, Casper said.

Square, I said.

Queer.

Whichever.

We finished the gin and had corn chips and dip and finally I said I'd best get my buttocks to bed, and what about him, Casper, didn't he work any more? No, it was Wednesdays off and Saturdays now; somebody had to keep the shit flowing Sunday. I could see he wasn't wanting to leave. His little house in the flats was a mess, prone to mold and mildew, and he and his wife, a huge fat Mexican woman, didn't have a thing to say to each other. Their daughter had moved off decades ago and rarely called. The last Casper knew she lived in Las Vegas.

Eventually he got up to go.

Seen any snakes? he asked.

Nope.

It's cause they're all run over now.

I had my hand on the doorknob; I might have yawned.

If I see one I'll send it down.

You do that, he said.

I fed the fish and washed dishes and turned some lights off, then went up to check on the kids. To the left in my standing-room attic stood the black boxes, eight altogether, for getting seeds started. The hydroponic self-feeder matrix (my purchase) sprawled beyond that, a network of plant cribs and plastic faucets and pipes. Far in the back the air filter squatted, and beside it my dryer, a great gray and white thing, for the sake of quick curing. The kids quivered in ecstatic clumps, happy to bursting under their lamps, 600-watt, high-pressure sodium bulbs, each plant in its moist shit- and humus-rich pot. They were thicker and lusher than any we'd had until now, all electric-green buds, outlandishly fat, streaked with dark purple, mahogany, cherry. I checked each pot for too dry and too moist and read the pH and adjusted the humidifier. Nearly ready, they were. Less than three weeks till harvest. We needed our buyer, or buyers, lined up; Bob and I needed to talk. I noticed the temperature'd dropped, even up here. The night had cooled off with the fog. Not a problem, these kids were tough, were in fact full-grown adults; and true potheads said a little autumn chill at the end made the poison more strong.

At the outset, the thought of getting caught with my pot scared me shitless. I dreamt about SWAT teams descending, storming in with assault guns and armbands; copter beams scanning; tall, vengeful bonfires on which cops tossed my uprooted trees. But the fear had subsided pretty much. I was cautious, I did my research, and didn't talk, didn't boast about the harvest or haul. Unlike my son, I had no record, not even a traffic ticket these last twenty years. Bob had cooked up a story, too, in case we got caught. My ancient aunt in Santa Rosa was ailing, this was no lie, and needed pain medication, true also; the herb therefore was hers, and we were its caretakers.

For Bob, of course, all this was business. A way to boost his savings, sizable already, and have a few pounds to share each year with his friends and to smoke. For me it was different. At the start, the crops were a way to grow worthy of Fudge, to nudge up my net worth. To impress my intended, my golden beloved, though I didn't dare then consider her that. They were all still this, yes, but now something else also. I liked standing neck-deep in my woods, telling the kids they were good, they were lovely and plump, outrageously pretty. I liked talking to Bob in code on the phone, when we did. *The kids outgrew their diapers this week. Time to change. Can you come by with wipes?* I liked the magazines, the web sites, the stoned friends I met online in chat, phantoms with routers and aliases; I liked the club I was in. I liked all the seeds, the names of the seeds and the plants they became. *Isis, Voodoo, God's Treat, Diablo, Durban, Pluton and Romulan Haze, Strawberry Cough, Nepalese Grizzly, Donkey Dick, Grape Skunk, Big Sticky.* I was working even now to create my own breed, my own special kid, a hybrid never seen before on the planet, a cross between *Thai Lights* and *First Lady*. *Fuma con Diós,* it would be called, in honor of poor Casper's wife. And of Kay, who I'd mostly forgiven, and all those who were needy.

I liked it very much, from seed to seedling to vacuum-sealed bag. I liked being sneaky. So much so that I had a problem. I'd been away from Kay for so long I didn't know if I knew a way back—to live with and love someone, truly. Despite pies and houseplants, despite my very real wish to unite and not gnash my teeth here on my own anymore, despite crosswords and toasts and wit and fresh fish and the sound of the sea hitting land, the most forlorn and lovely sound, surely, so lulling, known ever to woman or man.

By the time I got to the welcome-back party, everybody was there: Casper and Hammond and Leo B. Jensen, the widow and Bob, and Tom Russell too, the Vietnam vet, with his stare and farting prosthetic leg. As promised, there were refreshments galore: a case of Pete's Wicked Ale, a case of Bud Ice, a twelve-pack of Coors. I tied my hooks and weight on and cast out, then uncapped a Pete's. The fog was thick, making things fuzzy; you could hardly see who you saw down the dock. We had an incoming tide, higher than usual, and with it came fish. Bob was landing one now, not his first; he had nine or ten perch on his stringer, both rainbow and silver.

Kinda too little to keep, Casper observed, standing near.

Bob tied the thing on his stringer—rope end into mouth, out at the gill—and dropped the mess back in the bay. He'd lost weight, for sure. He looked worn, vaguely addled, and pale, though not without color. The foghorn was sounding, way out at the point.

Most of them's babies, said Casper.

Where's that whiskey? Bob answered.

Chuck, where's that whiskey? Casper said.

I handed Casper the bottle in its brown paper bag. Casper handed the bottle to Bob. Bob cast out again and his bobber dove right off. He set the hook, reeled. Hammond was reeling in also, pole curled toward the water. The fog thickened. You couldn't see boats, you couldn't make out the sea wall. Leo sank on his stool, pole in hand, drowsing, just beyond Bob. The widow sat on Casper's bright yellow cooler, wearing her fleece. The fog made her look gauzy, ethereal, ghostly. She watched Bob uncap the whiskey and drink. Old Overholt Rye. Something somebody might order in a western saloon, in Cheyenne or in Tombstone, home of the OK Corral.

Bob, what have you learned?

Too much, Lady Fudge.

There's never enough of too much.

Too much is too much, he said.

The bay lapped at the dock. Bob added his latest perch to the stringer. The foghorn moaned. Casper had a slug of whiskey, made a face and chased it with beer, then handed the bottle to Hammond. The baked goods were already out of the bike basket and bag. Muffins this time. Carrot-bran muffins, it looked like. A paper muffin-skin sat by Casper's foot, ridged, an ashtray for raisins, which he'd picked out. He didn't like raisins; sweet balls of bat shit was the phrase that he used. I finished my Pete's and started another and had a gulp or two of whiskey. I had no idea what I could or should say to Bob. He was still in charge here, still the crown prince of perch, impervious, if pale; and this was no place really to probe or make up. Just sitting here not saying anything, or not much, would help, I guess I was thinking. I was the same as I always was, he'd see, and not a conniving two-timer, the son of a bitch bastard he'd like me to be.

Down the dock, Hammond laughed with Tom Russell, all but invisible. The fog kept swirling in. Time's fun when you're having flies, Bob sighed. The fish kept hitting. Casper ran out of anchovies and had to borrow from me. A gull was shrieking on a piling somewhere. I caught four perch and a hefty jack smelt and let them all go. Tom Russell's leg farted. At least he'd have liked us to think it was his leg. Bob tipped the whiskey again, doing his Clint Eastwood routine. He held up his empty slimy bait bag.

Looks like we're about out, he said to me in Clint's voice, with Clint's face.

Pretty near, I said, doing the cowpuncher partner.

Winter's coming. Got them crops bundled up?

Yep.

Wife safe? Kids tucked in?

You bet.

Hammond and Tom sidled over, ready for another Bob drama.
Widow Fudge grinned. Casper was beaming. Fishing wasn't fishing,
evidently, without him, without us—without the Bob and Chuck
thing. Leo was out, dead asleep, chin on chest, pole drooping.

Partner, Bob said, I hear you're pretty good with your hands.

Better than some, I replied. Who said?

The widow did.

Widow who?

Fudge. She was hoping you'd, well, pull her out a tube worm.

Our audience roared. This was the way to melt conflict away,
obviously. Just drown it in comedy, in burlesque and charade, and
beer and rye whiskey. Even if it felt wrong to me; crass, vaguely
vengeful, unkind.

I'll get her the biggest tube worm she ever saw, I said.

More roaring. Cackles, guffaws. I got down on all fours in the
fog and peered along the dock, the submerged dock edge, where
tube worms lurked. I moved along, looking. Casper and Hammond backed out of my way.

Somebody get this man a saddle, Bob ordered.

What for? I said, my arm underwater now—I'd spied a clump,
a worm colony.

For the lady. So the widow can ride.

Not funny, Widow Fudge said.

You ride well, I hear, said Bob.

That's enough, said the widow.

There's never enough of enough.

Enough, she said.

I tugged and tore at the dock, my shoulder and neck and then
face in the water, and finally pulled a monster clump up, a foot
across and half again as tall, a streaming bouquet of gray shanks
topped with purple flowers, mock flowers; each was camouflaged at
the top to look like a plant, rather than the very tasty worm it was. I
unbuttoned my sleeve and wrung my shirt out, the part below the

elbow at least. I'd cut my forearm, I saw. My knuckles were bleeding. The salt water stung.

I hadn't heard what else they said, the widow and Bob, but the widow looked pissed. Hammond and Russell had moved off a bit. You had to know Bob well to know he was drunk. He didn't sink the way most people do. His concentration grew, he got philosophical, he took on roles, his nose got more red. He got sharper and clearer, like a blade getting whetted. And he got mean, I might add. He'd get meaner yet too, I knew, before he was done. I knew him; I knew how it went. He straightened on his stool, sighing.

Did I offend?

Just leave off, the widow said, popping the top on a beer.

I can leave, Bob said.

Come on, Casper said, eyeing Bob's fish.

Robert, she said, if you were my husband I'd poison your coffee.

Lady, he answered, if you were my wife, I'd probably drink it.

He rose and slid the pole out of Leo's hands and reeled it in. Then plucked a sheet of cheesecloth from his tackle box and wrapped Leo's muffin in it, his untouched carrot-bran muffin, and swabbed the whole thing in the pool of yellow-green blood on the dock where we'd been cutting tube worms. He squeezed the biggest worm from the clump and tucked the purple anemone head in at the muffin's one end and the creamy green tail at the other. It looked like a strange little sea snake that had swallowed something horrendously big—something it had no right to eat, and could not digest. Bob swabbed it all in worm blood again, and drew the pole back, muffin-snake dangling, and cast the thing out, out into the fog. The sound of the splash said it flew very far. Far into the channel, out past the sea wall.

In the meantime, right beside me, Casper was undoing Bob's stringer, releasing Bob's fish. I started to say something, and then didn't. He'd bent down and untied and now carefully stirred the nylon rope, the close end. And off they went, slowly. Bob stuck the pole back in Leo's hands as before, and loosened Leo's drag, and looked up and saw what Casper was doing. What Casper did.

Fucker Casper! Bob said.

The fish had swum off, all except one, which was swimming sideways by the surface in a drunk sort of circle, its belly stark white.

They were babies, Casper said, standing up.

They were *mine*.

Well, now they're nobody's.

The gull was shrieking again. Other gulls joined in the shrieking. Hammond and Tom hung in the fog past Widow Fudge, leaning in like a silent ghost chorus. The foghorn was moaning. Somebody was scraping and sanding somewhere in the marina.

Casper, you're not only dumb but you stink.

Leave him alone, I said.

Eat shit, said Bob.

You men are behaving like children, the widow said.

He stinks. He smells like a cesspool. At least he could bathe.

You don't eat them anyway, I said to Bob, meaning fish. They sit in your fridge and they rot.

At this point Leo's drag clicked, then buzzed. Hammond whacked Leo on the back and woke him and Leo stood up. Leo's drag buzzed and buzzed. Casper looked like he might cry. And then did.

You don't know shit about me, Bob said, stepping across.

I know enough.

Boys, knock it off, said the widow.

Hammond tightened Leo's drag and Leo tried pulling, looking like this was all just daily routine, like he caught monster fish all the time using bran muffins, deaf or not and half-blind, hair in his ear holes. Casper was crying, wiping his face with his sleeve.

I'd had it with Bob, finally. With the way he succeeded without even trying, and with not needing money and still taking mine, king of the dock or my attic or Negri's, wherever. I'd had it with him tormenting Casper. Who did smell, okay, but couldn't help it;

the sewer was in his pores, I suppose. Bob got first crack too at the widow. She'd have been mine otherwise, and we'd have been spared this. This ugliness. This ungainly wrestle.

What do you know? Bob said, standing next to me.

I know you're not the boss.

And I know you're not a thief. A backstabber.

Hammond took Leo's pole from him and worked it a minute and handed it back. Leo pulled and reeled and reeled and pulled; just another day at the dock for Leo B. Jensen. He tottered momentarily. Hammond reached to steady him. He stuck a finger in Leo's belt loop in back and held on.

Yes, I am, I told Bob.

We were both watching Leo's pole now, and Leo.

Yes you are what? Bob asked.

A backstabbing thief.

No, you're not.

I am.

Bob looked at Leo, then me.

You wish. You're just trying the part on for size. It doesn't fit.

About now Leo's fish came into sight, easing out of the depths. A mighty thing, colossal, a fish to behold. A gargantuan halibut. A long flattened fat garbage can, way too big for this dock, or for Leo, or twenty-pound line.

Jesus tits! Hammond cried.

The thing rose to the top as Bob and I looked, drifting up leisurely, easy and graceful and slow, gray and brown speckled, its undercarriage shock-white, and got a load of Leo, its monofilament master and lord, and of us all, seven gaudy clowns crowding in, and did something like laugh, and shook its massive fish face sideways and snapped Leo's line, and back down it went.

———

So once again Bob and I didn't fish, though the rest of them did. For a while they all used steel leaders, and muffins and tube worms for bait. Maybe Hammond crowned himself interim king.

I don't know. I didn't go. I did call Bob to do what I could, though, or try. I felt bad, cut off and snubbed as I was. He'd been first and foremost in my life after Kay. My sun and nutrition, my principal staple. I kept calling. He wouldn't answer, and then did. We talked on the phone finally. We had a week to go then till harvest, Bob and me and the kids.

He seemed ready partly to forgive and forget, as they say. We talked for ten or twelve minutes. But all wasn't right. He came across sounding forced on the phone, falsely complacent. He was playing the part of a friend, it felt like, who'd forget and forgive, given time and genuine sorrow from me. He was playing the part while watching it and us from a height. Still, he said he'd be out Thursday next to help cut and dry and seal-a-meal parcels. It looked like we had three buyers this time.

Meanwhile the widow was stirring Power Bait into her batter and pre-wrapping the muffins in cheesecloth. They nailed a few halibut actually and a big stingray or two. Including a forty-pounder for Casper, which tried to slip off, they said, by the dock; but the widow had her gun out this time, her ancient Doc Holliday pistol, and shot the thing dead. Honest to God. And it slid peaceably up, too big for the net.

What I didn't know was that Bob was making it up with the widow as well as with me. I learned all this later. Bob called and asked how she was, what had she learned, how life went with Chuck, what were our plans. She didn't want to hate him any more than I did. The man was infinitely lovable, even at his nastiest. So she told him how she was, and called him an ass and told him Get a life and grow up, and told him what we were doing. And not long after that, just before harvest, she and I left for San Fran.

We hadn't been anywhere yet except out to eat or to the dock or one of our houses. The trip was just what we needed, a sweet couple of days, even if she wouldn't let me pay for anything. We saw a play at the Geary, a comedy, British, about men taking other men's wives, brutally witty, men dressed in wigs and breeches and tights. We went to Fort Point and down to the pier by the seals, ate chocolate and oysters and sourdough bread, and walked arm-in-arm over the bridge. The fog burned off as we walked and the whole glorious skyline came into view: Nob Hill and Coit Tower, the Ferry building, the Bank of America and the what's-it-called building, shaped like a pointy pyramid—and way west, the cliff and sea coast and Palace of the Legion of Honor. For the first time in weeks I stopped thinking about him. About Bob, my ex-friend. I'd just bid on the Jenner house too, and was waiting to hear. Before we got back my bid was accepted. I'd just need to come up with the cash and be approved by the bank.

But what we found, coming back, changed all this. Changed everything. It was the last thing I imagined might happen. No, we didn't come home to a fire, or flood, or cops swarming my driveway and house. We didn't come home to news of Bob offing himself in his bathtub, or driving off the cliff in his truck, for the sake of lost love and friends. We were just stopping in to get clothes and shave cream for me, on the way to her place in Shell Beach. We didn't come home to more termites, or Kay sitting naked at the kitchen table with a bib on. No. What we came home to was—

Burglars, I said.

Oh my God, the widow said, stepping in.

We'd driven nearly three hours north to find this. To find my front door smashed, my cabinets and drawers hanging open, my computer gone and printer and TV and stereo, though the speakers remained. They'd taken these, along with my gin and bourbon and half my CDs. But the job looked unfinished. They'd lost nerve, it seemed. Or more likely, had opened drawers and carted stuff off for show, for effect. I knew right away what they'd come for and who was behind it. I'd been smacked, it felt like. Kicked in the guts. And such was my heartbreak and shock, I headed for the attic too soon. The widow followed me. I tried to pass it off, post-lapse, but well, there it was.

What's this? she said.

We'd scaled the stairwell, past the kicked-in little door, the portal, no secret now, and stood in the scatter of dirt and broken pots.

I couldn't have told her not to come up; my goose was cooked either way. She examined my futuristic quick-grow machines. Grow charts hung on the walls. Stacks of magazines, tipped over, stepped on, lay splayed by her feet.

A science project, I said.

I see.

Guess they didn't like it.

No, I'd say not.

And so it went. The whole ball game. They'd yanked every last one of my plants. My inconceivably beautiful plants. They'd even brought my garbage bags up from downstairs to stuff them in. The roll was unrolled on the floor like a long flat black tapeworm, or a funereal streamer. My stomach felt odd and my head went fuzzy. I thought I might have to lean over the john.

Maybe they liked it too much, the widow said.

Maybe, I told her.

We stood gaping at the mayhem a minute. I picked a leaf out of the dirt. And sniffed it, and held it.

This must have cost you, she said.

So I withdrew the bid on the house of my dreams. Our dreams, whatever those were: my dream of the dream the widow had, might have had, would keep having with me, both of us dreaming one dream. No house now. No dream. No wide wooden wraparound deck, no view of Goat Rock, no river flowing into the sea, no tracking sea lions with binoculars, the fat bulls with tusks, the pups they stepped on sometimes; no lines of migrating whales in the shimmering dawn. We were back to talk and no action and now she knew why. I'd improved my house, and spent a share of my gold on my new spiffy truck. There was no way the bank would approve me, not now. Not without that monster down payment I'd hoped to boggle them with.

What's more, I think I lost my resolve, or heat, my forward momentum, right there and then. There in my attic, and after, driving out to her house. Maybe she'd have still had me, I think now. She might still have loved me, sneaky or not. She might have really seen who I was and not let this lapse get between us. I believe she believed in me. But who can say? What's certain is I lost luster suddenly, not in her eyes so much as my own. I saw myself as I was and didn't like it. I saw something diminished. Something torn, something un-whole or undone.

So we did things less often. We saw less of each other. Finally she sold all she had and moved south, south to Cayucos, where the weather was warmer, the coast tamer, the hills less fierce on her joints and the wind less hostile to her skin. I suffered over this, yes, I felt stunted and fallow for weeks, but I wasn't wrecked. Even before she left I was making provisions. By spring I was dating new women. I wound up with a woman from Graton with a twelve-year-old son, which seemed a good thing; later we moved in together. There was less trying on my part with her, less vaunting, less bit-ing wit. But Widow Fudge got me started this way. She was my first post-Kay endeavor, and I loved her, odd love that it was. She got my courage up and whatever, got me back on the road of hoping to comprehend women. She opened the floodgates, set me loose on the tide, and in spite of my setback I'd still see lights in the dark I was in and go on.

In the end Casper was the only one left who fished. Wednesdays or not, it didn't matter. Leo had a stroke at the dock one afternoon; they thought he'd choked on one of the widow's white chocolate cookies. Hammond crashed his van into someone's guest cabin in Guerneville and got his license pulled, his third or fourth DUI. Casper dragged me to Bodega twice a year or so nonetheless. The last time we went somebody said, Did you know this dock's private, and Casper said, Yes, but we're friends with Bob. And that settled that.

Casper stayed my neighbor too, though I sold my house and moved. I bought another house in Camp Meeker, on the same road, just higher up the mountain is all, with more sun and more view. The woman from Graton and I and her boy ate steaks and berry pies on my deck at dusk and slapped at mosquitoes and watched movies beamed in by satellite. And little by little I began to forget about Bob. To mostly forget about Bob. What had I learned? Plenty, and not nearly enough. He's just a speck now on the glass of much clearer vision, I wish I could say. He still lives eight miles away, on his own hill, between the woods and the coast, and grates at me, though I haven't seen him, except in passing, unspeaking. I wonder which new dupe he might be misleading now. Who the new dildo might be, and what the payment on his part will be for defiance.

I haven't grown a thing either since I was robbed. I haven't dared. I figured Bob would raid me again for the sake of his grudge. And Bob can nurture a grudge, it appears. But it's been a few years, and spring's coming. I miss it. Cultivating, that is. This house is bigger, more spacious, better ventilated, with more natural light. My woman from Graton was a hippie once too, not unlike Bob; and her son, fifteen now, smokes the stuff in his room and she doesn't stop him—and wouldn't stop me, or mind all that much, I'd like to think. Fall might be hard, I admit. I mean those late weeks of autumn. Those hours before harvest. I might not look like the type to sit in the dark all night with a loaded gun aimed, night after night, waiting. But I will if I have to, if it comes to that. And after all these years of waiting to cry I might just cry as I do it. As I play me in my life, not a pawn in some game, not a bit part in somebody's drama, not prey to saviors or snakes or kidnappers. As I unseat him, as I erase him, as I blindly blow him away.

Hers

Problem is it's cold outside, her fingers don't work like they should, and she can't think which secret pocket she stuck the keys in, if it was even this jacket. She finds her Kleenex, her toenail clipper, a red rubber bone. Todd, her dog, squirms on Edgar's arm. Edgar has to set the suitcase down on the drive, though it's wet.

Mom, let me drive, he says.

I told you no.

Todd yips, squirming again.

Well, let's get in at least.

Hold your frickin horses.

They're on their way to the hospital. To Kaiser, in town. Edgar isn't happy about this. He's been reading things on his computer as usual. A gallbladder's like a tonsil, his computer insists. They don't yank tonsils out anymore; that, they say now, was barbaric. The same goes for gallbladders—or it will, he says, when people wake up. But she does what her doctor says, period. She's sick of this burn and ache in her guts. She's sick of yellow eyes, and the diaper. And Edgar's no doctor. Her doctor's the doctor.

She unlocks the car door finally. Edgar slips her bags in back and drops Todd on his plaid dog blanket. Todd snaps the blanket up with his teeth and shakes it, snarling, too cute almost for his britches. She turns the engine on, and the heat. Edgar stands brushing dog hair off his sweater, then gets in. He's got his undertaker's expression on, like he just sucked a half-dozen lemons. The fan blows cold air at her feet.

I hope we know the way, he says.

Edgar, don't start.

Just so we don't get confused.

I know what's what.

But you get confused.

I do not get confused.

The last time something happened he took her car keys away. She had to call a locksmith and lie and say she lost her keys, could he make more, and the job wasn't cheap. She had the guy make multiple sets, actually. She's got keys stashed all over the house now; she can't help but find a spare set, wherever they are, if it comes to that.

Let's go, Edgar says.

In her day, a person warmed a car up. It doesn't seem right to just get in and drive, despite Edgar's facts, whatever advice he has to prescribe. Warming the engine, she tries to find gum, but the gum's in her purse and her purse is in the back and she can't reach like she used to, her body's so stiff—but she needs it, the gum, since she smoked before, smoked in fact for forty-six years, she always smoked when she drove, but now she can't, she quit, they made her quit, smoking, not driving, and only—

What? Edgar asks.

She tells him Gum. He sighs. Then leans back for her purse, belly pulling the buttons on his businessman's shirt, his freckled bald spot pointing her way. Todd does his dance, grinning, panting, standing on tiptoe for Edgar, his little hands on Edgar's shoulder. Simply too cute! That peach and cream fur on his face! Those bulgy eyes, and eye and lip liner! She paid a hideous price at the pet shop but what a sweet dog. And not stinky, no matter what Edgar says. Todd's blanket might stink just a little. It smells like Todd. And Todd is a dog, and a dog can't help but smell like a dog.

Edgar gives her the gum. She takes a stick and hands the pack back to him, saying, Gum? but he doesn't want any. She stuffs the wadded wrapper in the ashtray. She checks her hair in the mirror, revving the engine. All she'd done that day was take a wrong turn and head for Sparta, or was it Rock Lake? She called her niece to ask where she was, and her niece called Edgar's wife, who called Edgar, and there lay her error; she'd have to watch her ass better.

I'm keeping it, she tells him now.

He looks at her.

The car?

My organ. Gallbladder.

You're keeping your gallbladder.

Yes.

That's very nice.

I got a coffee can out to stick in the freezer.

Good, Mom.

Your father's tumor's still in there, God rest his carcass.

Why don't you ease up on the gas?

She lifts her right foot a bit and the roaring dies back. She looks at him. The fan keeps belting out air. Edgar stares out the windshield. The garage door is pale green, the same color almost as her dress, which she got for half price at Blair.

He's a good son, it's true. He calls to see how she is, he comes by to eat or help her clean house or mow and weed whack, he sprinkles the crystals under her rhododendrons. He brings videos over, which they watch, she and Edgar and Todd. He surprises her with bagels, or a cake from the bakery, or See's candy. He says let's do the garage, and they begin, but there's too much to sort, all those boxes of pictures and papers and books and knickknacks, stools and plant stands and lamps and who knows what else, dog toys, embroidery, kites, even his father's golf clubs, God rest his dead ass, which she can't quite give up. Who says it's wrong for a car to just sit in the driveway?

He is a good son. So good he pisses her off, wielding his knowledge and youth, even if what hair he's got left is gray as hers is these days. And that smartass computer! Or that tragic look he gets on his face—it makes her furious! Like this might be the last time he'll see her!

I'll be picking you up tomorrow, he tells her now.

She tips the rearview down to see Todd, who stands with his little chin on the window edge, making his nose prints.

In my car, I mean, Edgar says. I just don't think you should drive.

She guns the gas again.

What'll you do, take it to Fairfax and sell it?

Your organ?

My car.

He looks across, then away.

Well—yes. We did find a buyer, actually.

He looks both shocked and relieved, like this was exactly the thing he'd wanted to say but not the place nor the right time to say it. She turns the fan down on the dash.

You sold my car.

We got better than blue book. The money's yours.

She looks in the mirrors and checks her seatbelt. Edgar stares straight ahead.

So it had come down to this. The next thing she'll hear is her house is for sale. Isn't that how the old story goes? Then it's off to Rolling Acres or Greenbrae, assisted living with the bedwetting loonies, cold gruel and pills and turds flying, nonstop weeping and screaming. Todd will end up adopted, he'll be beaten and kicked, left to sleep in his own piss in a cage. In the meantime, of course, she'll be stuck. She'll be at Edgar's mercy completely. She'll have to depend on Trudy, her neighbor, that fat old bitch, that battle-axe.

And on the van that comes to cart the pissants around, the geezers and drips and shit-butts with walkers.

She undoes the emergency brake, slips the shift knob down.

We don't want you killing yourself, Mom.

Don't you Mom me, she says.

She turns, tries to crane her neck to look but her neck is too stiff and they're rolling now anyway, slipping down the drive backward, and maybe too quickly. She hits the brake hard. Instead of stopping short like a decent car should the thing jolts ahead, or does it, who can say, who can think in the cracking once the chaos begins? The garage door is kindling and the kitchen wall too, and now the wall to the den, but who'd notice, it happens so fast, who'd see the roof caving in, collapsing on plant stands and puzzles and shattered antiques, croquet mallets and kites, on eight generations of china in pieces, her water dispenser upended, the coffee can for the organ sitting quaintly upright. Besides, she's got an appointment, and motherfuck it she'll get there, by crook or by hook. Even if she has to circle back by Rock Lake, or Sparta, wherever. Even if there's a truck dead ahead on the road, and there is, wherever she is, bearing down in the dusk, hugely floodlit, a truck loaded with logs or with ice, aiming straight at her, bearing down on the car, which is hers.

Paradise Road

She sat at his wife's place at the table, wearing her clothes—his wife's clothes, that is. She ate a bit of carrot or two and a piece of potato, then picked the bowl up and drank, and pushed it his way and told him to finish, saying she'd had enough. He carried the bowl off and came back with a big plate of cookies. He refilled her milk, saying she could stay if she liked. He didn't know what he expected or what he was thinking. It was the way her eyes lit up when he set down dessert. She seemed normal all of a sudden.

So why's Cindy so mad? she said, meaning his wife.

I haven't been good, he said. I'm not nice.

But you *are* good. You *are* nice.

How did she know, he asked. She had Cindy's big red sweatshirt on, a pair of Cindy's white socks pulled to her kneecaps.

I just know, she said, and reached for a cookie.

He met her on Paradise Road, where she'd been walking half-naked. This was no lie. He came up the trail, fish pole and tackle in hand, and, well, there she was, traipsing along, blond, bone-skinny, nothing on but a pair of old cutoffs. She knew where he lived; she'd made friends already with his horses, down the hill by the fence. Aren't you freezing? he asked. It was forty degrees out, or less. Cold was no problem, she said—when you use all your skin, you feel spring coming on.

Poor, fat horse, she said now, glancing around, chewing her cookie. Outside, the mare stood beside her gray-muzzled husband the stallion, pregnant as shit, fading in twilight there at the feeder. Steam rose from their noses.

Poor fat horse nothing, he said. That horse had it better than he did, actually. The teakettle whistled. Coffee? he said.

The girl just stared out the window. He noted her profile, the smooth hills of her breasts. Her hair was lopped abruptly at the jawline. She'd said she was twenty, but looked eighteen; younger, God help her and the world. She'd been staying up the hill with the monks at this Buddhist Gumby or Gumdrop, whatever they called it, a towering gold and red pagoda-roofed thing; she'd worn out her welcome, evidently.

When'll the baby be here? she asked. She meant the colt, or the filly.

Next week. Anytime, really.

So she's gone for goods-ville?

He set the coffee down on the table. A quart of whole milk, some sugar.

Who?

Cindy.

I don't know. I suppose.

Her toast lay cold on the napkin, a single corner nibbled off. The chicken leg in her bowl looked like a thing washed up by the river.

You poor man, she intoned.

Poor man nothing, he told her.

She drank half her coffee then bounced up and yawned, and smiling like a girl caught in a lie, said, Can I take a bath?

By the time he pulled a fresh towel and washcloth out she had her clothes off again. All of them. He got the water started in the tub, showing her how to shut off the faucet, then lifted his wife's blue box of bath soap from the cabinet. She eased into the water. Bones stuck out on her shoulders. He could count all her ribs.

He washed the soup pot and dishes, stoked the woodstove, put his pole and tackle away and sat down by the tube. He got all of three channels, not much to choose from—tonight it was a movie he'd seen already and a sitcom and some glitzy celebrity nonsense. He turned the thing off and picked up the paper, but couldn't concentrate any better on that. A guy didn't have young women stripping in his house every night, smiling these provocative smiles. Women didn't just fall in your lap, or follow you home.

Okay, she wasn't beautiful, exactly. She wasn't ugly, either. Just skinny, and damaged somehow, half-crazy, lost. He got up to feed the horses, passing the open door of the bathroom on his way out. She'd slid down in the tub, knees up, wet washcloth draped on her face. Drops dripped at the faucet. She might've been asleep, she was so still.

The moon shone on his pickup, his split-rail fence, the sloping concrete walk to the barn and tool shed and squash frozen dead in the garden, the ragged cutouts of alder and pine. He plucked a chunk of hay from the bale, there by his mountain of cordwood and his starter-wood box, the neat thin splints of kindling. He tossed the hay over and reached through the fence to pour the sticky grain on. The mare'd already laid into her meal. Her husband, the stallion, slumped a few paces off, waiting his turn. If he moved up too close, she'd bite him.

He was no horse-nut himself. In fact he'd always thought they were weird: tube-faced, pop-eyed, bony and edgy, apples of shit plopping out from behind. But these were Cindy's leavings, her hide and blood residue. She'd been gone now three months. All she took was her money and keys and the clothes she had on; she left nary a note, not even an I've had it you bastard or Fuck you, I'll see you in court. He'd been caretaking her horses, her winter garden, her clothes. He stood there a minute watching the mare,

Cindy's mare, eat. Voices crisscrossed the breeze. His neighbors the Buddhists had a function in progress, and the chanting was wafting, extraterrestrial-strange, through the trees.

Before he turned building inspector he did construction. He'd built this house he lived in with the help of his then soon-to-be-brother-in-law Ken, with whom he'd been on especially good terms. Ken introduced him to Cindy, in fact, thinking they'd get along, and they did. Ken wasn't happy to see his sister deceived, needless to say. So when the phone rang tonight Don didn't pick up, supposing it was Ken again calling from a bar in Redding, half-crocked, to call him a dingus, a fuck brain, a dork. Calling to say if he, Don, ever messed with Cindy again he'd be outrageously sorry. That is, if he lived.

The phone rang five times, six, then the voicemail kicked in. Outside, one of the horses let out a snort. The girl crept up the hallway, steaming just slightly. She had a burgundy towel wrapped on her body.

Bedtime, she said.

He led her down to the guest room, clicked the lamp on and tugged the cord for the curtains. He drew the covers back on the bed and folded the sheets in a triangle. His brainless pecker responded, butting its head on his pants.

Sleep as long as you need to, he told her.

Bedtime, the girl said again, pink-cheeked. Then sighed, unwrapping the towel, and drew her thin legs in under the covers, and wriggled around like a nine-year-old, fluttering against the cold sheets. Her hair shone, shiny and damp on the pillow. In the lamplight he saw freckles on her cheeks and nose. He hadn't seen them before.

You be sure she's eighteen first, he said to himself. No ID, no entry. Besides, the girl was a loon. He could hop in and ram her, fine, but where was the challenge? It'd be like running a dash against a man in a wheelchair. Why not hold his resolve? That was the main thing. He'd been celibate ten weeks already. A record for him. He'd been trying to change. He'd honestly tried. He'd stopped going to bars and stopped flirting, almost. He'd ruined his marriage, and others, too, in the process, and needed to stop. He'd had a good youth. He'd been with plenty of women. In Chico once he'd had three different girls in one day, all at different places and times. He'd been with a black girl, a Filipina, a squat Guatemalan, a sweet compact beauty from Laos. What more did he want? He'd done a lot. But he'd never slept with a dingbat or a child. At least he could draw the line there.

You're a nice man, the girl said. Her gray eyes clamped on his and held on. Why don't you answer the phone?

He sat down on the bedside and said, I don't believe in the phone.

I'll answer it, then. Can I?

No way, he said.

There was something about the way she paused when she spoke, as if thoughts would float in and disrupt. She gazed at him now, somehow present and vacant at once. She looked about as haunted and dead as he felt.

Sleep now, he said.

He leaned over and pressed his lips to her temple, at war with his hormones and the bulk of his past. When she tilted her face to bring her lips up to his, he pulled away.

———————

He'd been writing to Cindy. So far the letter had taken a month and was nowhere near finished. Not that he intended to write her a phone book, spilling his guts for ten thousand pages; he just couldn't get the few pages he did want to send to sound right. He'd reworded this and chopped out that, just to cross it all out from word one and start over. He wrote even now, driving back from Burnt Ranch and Del Loma, winding east up the river, jabbering into his mini-recorder, which he'd replay later to add to the letter, and tinker and tear at and finally throw away, too.

This girl's been staying, he told the machine. She's from a place called Commerce. The City of Commerce, south of L.A. He didn't go on to explain that the mother had overdosed and died when the girl was seven. That the dad was a trucker (she'd never met him), that she'd been raised by her gramps, who, as she said, rarely bathed, and spent his days watching TV game shows and COPS, drinking grape juice and gin.

Down off the bank on the right, on a wet boulder by the river, a man stood fishing. Olive cap, camouflage jacket—Don caught a glimpse as he curved past the fork. He saw the man draw back to cast, the incandescent flash as the lure shot over the water. It had rained lately, the river had risen and dropped. It flowed milky green, the deeper holes darker, brooding, steelhead-ripe.

She was petting the mare, he told the recorder. He was lying a little, but who'd believe what really happened?

She saw woodsmoke, he said, and she came to the door. I let her warm up by the stove.

A semi flew by with a big load of pine logs. Sun shone on the pavement and double yellow line, the glistening snake-body of river and cliffs rising above. Sun made the wet tree branches sparkle.

I haven't touched her, he told Cindy now. I've changed. Ask her, she'll tell you. She'll just be here a while. Then she'll be gone.

He wouldn't leave in the stuff about Kim—the girl's name, incidentally. No way. If there was a last-spark chance in the dead fire of his marriage, that'd be the bucket of ice water to quell it. Which is to say he was just talking, not writing. He liked to talk about women. Women he'd been with, women he wanted. It was a tradition of sorts. Decades before, on the back page of a date book he started in college, he penned the names of the women he'd been with—not so many at that point, surely no more than twenty. The list grew; eventually he had to add extra paper. There were more than two hundred names there the last time he counted, some with details appended to help fire memory—where he met her, what she looked like, etc. For instance: *Patty. Dragon Moon. Slim Texas belle. Peed when she came.* He knew bodies, female bodies. He'd studied the G-spot and nuanced clitoris, he'd read Shere Hite and Masters & Johnson and Erica Jong. He knew about Tantra, these hours-long shuddering bouts, sensational valleys rather than peaks. Though no hippie himself, he bathed in the tide of the '60s and '70s, he let his hair fly, short hair or not, and swept along year after heavenly year, finally drowned and washed up.

What was sex anyway besides animal fire, exchanging fluids, pulsing naked hot flesh? Some tied it to original sin. Some thought it neither sin nor original. Suffice it to say that his first girlfriend dumped him, dropped him like a turd from a tall cow's behind, and he'd made amends ever since.

He shifted to third and passed the Quik Mart and laundromat on the outskirts of town. He passed the pair of gas stations and the deli and video store. Slowly he cruised past the supermarket and movie theater and bookstore and backpackers' outlet, eyes peeled—against his will, more or less—for good-looking women. In front of the organic grocery a woman his age stood in a puffy blue dress, gray hair hanging to her elbows. Beside her, gesturing, gripping a canvas bag at the handle, was a younger raven-haired woman. She wore faded jeans and a tight white T-shirt, wide silver hoops at her wrists.

For Don Juan, one fears, hell is wall-to-wall women, steaming and writhing, all crowding up groaning, sighing, taking tickets in line, and not one jot or tittle of pleasure to be had for the man, tears of despair blotting his handwritten list.

Cindy, I'm sorry, he said to the tape.

Instead of turning into his driveway, he drove on, on past his special trail to the river, farther up the asphalt channel between pines and sunny weedy green meadows to the neighbor's drive, which was muddy and steep; his wheels spun as he went. He pulled in and got out and stepped up and knocked. Nobody answered. A cat sat at one end of the porch, blinking, a big yellow-eyed black and white thing. A blue-belly lizard lay before it, dead or trying to pretend it was dead. He knocked again. Nobody, just the rush of wind in the lodgepoles high on the hill, the distant clamor of the river.

He didn't know these people at all. They'd been here only two years and kept to themselves. They were involved with the nuns and monks in some way, with the monastery, which attracted all manner of transient, zealot, oddball, and freak. It was only right, he knew, to let them know about Kim, this girl he'd adopted, or vice versa. And maybe check on her age—she didn't carry ID.

He checked the garage, a long open-faced leaky old structure. They had a regular woodshop set up inside, table saw, band saw, jigsaw, lathe. The right half they'd converted to quarters. Or she had, judging by what Cindy had said; the wife had been pounding and sawing for weeks. He stepped in and looked. An amateur job, construction-wise, and not legal, but not half-bad, actually. For the most part the seams were straight. The nails, unbent, were driven in in uniform lines. And this done by a middle-aged woman. On the walls were tall paintings, gods and dragons and such, red and bright orange and purple on black. A woven mat sat in one corner. And on a shelf at the head of the mat, a small gold Buddha, pot-bellied, smiling.

The door opened across at the house and the Chinese guy, the husband, stepped out. Don raised his hand and said hi, said he thought it was about time he stopped by to visit. The man ushered him in.

They lived in a double-wide that the former owners had sided over and added porches and sheds to, and basically made look like a house. The linoleum, scuffed and discolored, needed to be re-placed, the brown carpet was trampled; the veneer paneling might have cost twelve cents a foot. Don followed the man to the kitchen. The black and white cat strolled in behind. The sink and counters were cluttered with dishes. It smelled like an Italian eatery in there. Parmesan, basil, and garlic.

How is your wife? the man said. He wore baggy white cotton pants and plastic sandals, a pale yellow-green T-shirt. His shaved head was sprouting new hair.

She's gone. She's down seeing relatives.

Ah, the man said, and grinned. He pulled two cups from a shelf and then lifted a teapot. The place was freezing inside but the man seemed not to notice. A moth sailed out of a cupboard, one of these wicked little grain-eating types. They carried the cups to the living room. Magazines and books ranged in piles all around, stacked on the floor and end tables, on chairs. A computer glowed in one corner, an antiquated, outdated clone rising out of a blizzard of paper. The man half-bowed at a chair. Don sat down. His host sat on a stool.

Your horse is a mother, the man said.

Any time now. Late this week, I'd say. Friday.

Friday, he chimed, grinning.

The cat walked in from the kitchen, tail pointing straight up. A moth buzzed toward the sliding glass door. The tea tasted like weeds. Don glanced at the desk.

What're you working on here?

The man said he and his wife were compiling translated transcripts of the venerable lectures, the Ricochet's, whatever they called him, this prune-faced guy Don had seen on the flyers with the wise eyes and gray spaghetti whiskers. Don had had no idea what they were up to in here. All he knew was they walked each day up Paradise Road past his fence and over the bridge to the post office, alone or together, sometimes plodding through snow. She was a good six inches taller than him.

The phone rang. The man excused himself and slipped down the hall in his thongs to a bedroom. Don sat holding his teacup. On the wall by his head hung a picture of the man's wife and her daughter. The two stood arm-in-arm, faces millimeters apart, both sporting haircuts they called "shag" in the old days. The faces looked so alike they might've been sisters, the daughter a product of a former marriage, no doubt, whiter than white, white as her mother.

Ken and Don were partners of sorts about the time he met Cindy. In those days things seemed perfectly simple. Don had hurt his back on a job and was laid up; he sat around reading, watching movies, getting the files in order and so on, which is to say setting priorities straight: straight as they ever were anyway in his amusement-ride life. Ken ran things at the site—foundations, framing, electricians, inspectors, roofers, plumbers—while Don did the paperwork, relaxed, and recovered. On days off they fished. Or they went to the swap meet, or drove with six-packs to the coast, trading the obligatory vile jokes. They trekked to Eugene for the bluegrass festival. Ken was such a joker you couldn't resist him. Strangers would creep up to listen and scream when he made his animal sounds, the pig squeal or quarter horse whinny, the billy goat bleat; and when he barked like a seal, blaring from the pit of his guts, you'd want to throw him a fish.

Then Cindy fell into the picture. They started going around as a team. That time seemed a blur now, Don was so happy. For the first time he didn't feel hungry, so glad he felt just to be where he was and so completely in love he could die. Cindy was as funny as Ken was. She was bright, black-haired, and fit. She made love better than anybody else on this earth.

Three paces away, the cat sat hunched in a ball by the wood-stove—which was unlit, cold as the rest of the house—as if by the force of sheer concentration it could cause wood to ignite. The man's voice floated up from the bedroom. The words were Chinese.

Don wondered if the man had any friends. It might be just him and his wife out in the woods with their computers and Buddhas. The man might lack male company, he might need a guy to drink tea with. But no, he belonged to a church, that tall spaceship on the hill with its paper flags flapping and unearthly gongs. People in churches had all kinds of friends. For a second Don thought: maybe *he* ought to get involved in a church, meet people, kneel, try not to go crazy. Then he thought, sure, they'd know who you were, Mr. Inspector. He's here to meet women, they'd say, or they'd think, here to find some young holy bunny to lead off to the pasture. And they would be right.

It might be a comfort, he thought, to have a thing to believe in. Anything. Buddha, Vedanta, Isis, or Jesus. He'd walked the full length of plank over that shark tank of his values, his parboiled world. Did the Inspector have any kind of code of his own? Beyond the prescripts of pluck, and fear of sharp teeth?

The man appeared and took the cup from Don's hand and stepped out to refill it. And returned, handed it back. Don thanked him. The man sat down again, beaming. The cat peered over, sniffing, and yawned. Don asked the man if he knew this blond girl he'd met, and described her. He told the man she'd told him she stayed at the temple.

The girl who tries patience, the man said.

Tries patience?

That's what the Rinpoche called her, he answered. This child-woman who never finished her chores, disappeared if asked to help in the kitchen and couldn't concentrate long during sittings, group meditations. She exasperated fellow practitioners, who thrived on calm and dead silence. But the Master said she was useful. The world would distract no matter what, no matter how quiet you got. And here was proof. Proof they could work with.

She's gone now a little, the man said. Maybe for good.

Don had come to confess, but didn't want the man to think him the lech that he was. That he'd been.

She's around, he said.

You know her?

I've seen her.

The man studied Don's face a moment. A moth whizzed up and lit on his T-shirt. He cupped his hand underneath and flicked it onto his palm, then rose, opened the sliding glass door and, crossing the enclosed back porch—illegal also—let the thing go out a window. He stepped in and sat down again, grinning. He said his Master had wondered about her.

Where is girl who try patience? he said, doing his boss—a Chinese guy doing Tibetan bad English. He peered around. Where? he said. *Where?*

———

Back at the house the girl sat at the table. She'd poured herself a bowl of cereal. She was reading the box.

I thought you went fishing, she said. Where's your bucket?

Don unzipped his jacket.

Early riser, she said.

It was one-thirty in the afternoon. She had Cindy's red sweat-shirt on, nothing on underneath. She pushed the bowl away on the placemat, then pulled it back and raised it to her lips and drank out the milk. He felt like pulling her shirt up and leaning her over right there on the table. He felt like rubbing her all over with oil. Show him one man on this planet who wouldn't, except his neighbor maybe and his neighbor's whiskery master. He felt like spending three whole days in bed.

Get enough? he asked her, keeping his lewd thoughts in his pants. There's bread here for toast. And fruit. Have an apple.

The phone rang. He let it keep ringing. A jay lit on a branch outside, bluer than blue. It started to rasp.

I don't want an apple, she said.

What would you like, then?

A baby.

Jesus, he thought. The freckles were there on her cheeks again, in the pale sunlight.

Why, he said.

I just do.

They're a lot of work.

But I couldn't, she said. The doctor said I had to eat more or my eggs wouldn't, you know. Drop down and be fertile.

So eat, he told her.

I *do,* she said.

He called the vet in on Thursday and the nightmare began. The last thing he expected was that he'd show up with Ken. The vet and Ken were friends, yes, and Ken helped now and then. But Don couldn't believe Ken would actually come here and face him.

So down from the doctor's truck climbed Ken his brother-in-law, beardless now, slogging through mud and dung in his work boots. The doctor followed, armed with his long stained canvas bag of instruments, and went right to work, planting Ken at the head as the black blinder went on, inserting his own gloved hand at the back end, his forearm, his elbow; his whole arm disappeared. The mare puffed like a tractor, wheezing, blasting air in Ken's face, wet torso heaving.

It's okay, okay, Ken said, gripping her tight. He had a green and black flannel shirt on, new blue jeans. He looked naked without hair on his face.

The doctor slid his arm out, dug around in his bag, and said, Well, this ought to be easy.

Been catching fish? Ken said, glancing at Don.

Little one, couple weeks ago. Not much to catch.

The doctor walked back to his pickup. Don's bald neighbor moved up the road, straight-backed, same yellow-green shirt, slow and deliberate, as if in a trance. The mare puffed, steaming. Ken small talked; Don answered. For all his mock-easy carriage and backwoods bluster and jokes about to fly off his lip, Ken looked awkward as shit. Don had never seen him look awkward; he didn't think it could happen. What a deal for him to come out here, he thought. It had to be hard, he'd been a jerk.

Cindy back from her folks?

She never went. She just didn't want you around.

I don't blame her.

I don't either.

A car rolled by on the road. The doctor returned and poked the mare with a needle, stuck his arm in again. The mare grunted, flipped her head, stamped a front hoof. Okay, let's do it, the doctor said, and Ken said, Here, take her head, and moved alongside and began pushing the belly, timing his thrusts with the rhythmic contractions, and Don held the head while the vet reached and jerked and all at once it was out on the mud, flopping, a gooey primordial thing, spindle-legged, a soggy mini-giraffe, dark crimson and black, the steam rising in waves.

She's saying you might get one last chance, Ken said, still out of breath.

Don thought right then his chest would crack open. He'd kneel before this man now, if need be, all hard words erased, and say let's stay friends forever, and be nice, and drink to kinship and God and sing loud about love, and not blow it, never be sorry again: just stand me back up in the gaze of your sister. But that's when it happened. That's when the girl slipped out of the woods, gliding from shadow to sun, wearing nothing but a pair of Cindy's black panties.

Ken's jaw fell. The doctor gaped. The mare's head craned around, blindfold or not. They all stared at the girl. Her blond hair gleamed, her freckles stood out. Her nipples were stone-tight in the cold. She knelt in the mud by the colt.

Finally, she said.

She ran a hand over the broom-bristle mane and delicate snout. She looked at the slime on her hand; she raised it and sniffed. Then she stood up and smiled and walked off toward the house. The panties were big on her. She'd rolled them, pulling them high on her hips.

Ken stared. He shook his head and glared, then went out the gate and climbed in the truck. A Volkswagen rattled past on the road. Meanwhile the doctor inspected the colt and, acting as if nothing had happened, said that the fetlock had fused with the hoof. The colt was defective, in short. There wasn't one thing they could do, he said, except shoot it. The mare hovered over the creature, panting, licking its spine. Don's neighbor appeared again, floating along on foot. He paused, peering over the fence, and nodded, moved off. Music swirled up—Ken had turned the car radio on. Steel guitar and bass and low vocals. A country lament.

The doctor gave Don a full box of needles and vials, saying he'd have to inject the mare before he sat down to milk her, she'd be up-set. He said he was sorry, shook Don's hand, threw his bag in the truck; he said something to Ken and backed up and drove down the hill. Don led the mare to the barn and locked her in with the stal-lion, then went to the house for his gun. By the time he got back with the rifle she was slamming the barn floor with her hooves, snorting and stamping. The colt tried to stand. Don pressed the rickety legs down with his boot soles, pushed the damp nose to the earth, aimed, lifted the safety, aimed again, fired. The sound echoed and echoed, downriver and up. He looked across then and saw the girl at the window. Wide-eyed she stood, hands clutching her breasts. He dug a hole by the barn, stopping now and then to breathe, and finally slid the colt in and pushed the dirt over.

In the bedroom his wife's drawers were open. The closet door was ajar. The girl had taken a pair of leather moccasin-sandals, it looked like. Three or four T-shirts. The beloved red sweatshirt, some panties and socks. He pulled the closet door closed and shoved in the drawers and went to the kitchen to look for a note. He looked all over the house. Déjà vu. No note to be found.

Later he cheeseclothed roe into bait-packs and took his waders up and rod and set off to fish. On the way he let the horses loose in the yard. The mare ran in circles, out of her mind, shaking her mane and tail, rearing up.

The current was fierce, the milky river churning hard over rocks, rippling into the bend. Trees rose beyond, gray-green, fuzzy, staggered hill upon hill. After ten minutes a steelhead hit, but Don was too slow, he didn't yank up in time. Twenty minutes later he hooked something ridiculous, a log or a stump slipping along the bottom, and kept pulling and reeling and reeling and pulling, then his line snapped and the slack buzzed past his ear. He packed his things and started back. Halfway up to the road, a quarter mile from the house, the mare let out a bellow, the first of the bellows he'd be hearing for days, horrific outbursts. Like an ancient woman howling in pain, crossed with the sound of a transformer blowing.

As he walked west on Paradise Road in his waders someone cruised up behind.

Expecting a flood? Ben Heller said from his Bronco. Ben was a guy he'd see at the bar.

Don told him he hadn't caught shit, impatient to walk. Ben

called him a lying fuck and said, How many fish you got stashed in the freezer? then slipped his truck into neutral, pulled on the emergency brake. Don asked if he'd seen any women out walking naked.

Ben switched his truck off. You know this psycho chick, too? Tits hanging out in the weather?

Who.

Blond hair, skinny. Nice little butt. You seen her?

Maybe.

Cocksucker, Ben said, banging his hand on the steering wheel. You, too?

Don felt sick to his stomach. He broke down the rod he held in his hand; he hooked the snap-swivel onto the arm of the reel. Up the road the mare howled, the sound echoing out.

You old goat, Ben said, shaking his head. Howard met her at Percy's. Says she knows how to screw.

I just saw her walking.

Lying stinking sack of shit, Ben said, and laughed. You ought to learn how to lie. It's a wonder there ain't guys in line fishing your spot at the river.

Back at the house Don warmed his dinner and clicked the TV on. He took two bites of food and drank a half glass of milk then dropped it all in the sink and crawled into bed. He felt dead from feet to forehead. It was like he'd been stuck a dozen times in the gullet, or gut-shot, blasted point-blank. After a while he got up and took off his pants and shirt. He lay there trying to sleep, and couldn't. He'd fling the covers off, and then, freezing, tug them back over, then get up to drink water or go to the toilet. Up the hill the Buddhists were on an all-nighter, chanting and chanting, like ghosts piling straw against sleep, undercut by murmurs from women he'd damaged, their hearts stuffed with dust. The mare cut loose with a groan, a long deep-winded wail. By dawn he was ready to go shoot *it* in the head, and cut short the hysteria, misery. Either that or hold it close to his body, his face in its mane, and breathe its smell in, and weep.

At some point the phone rang. He picked it up before the first ring was done. Of course it was Ken. Hey, Shit Breath, he said, who are you fucking tonight? Then he squealed like a pig and hung up.

If she hadn't left on her own, Don would have had to tell her to leave. And he would've said, Here, let there be commerce, or better yet, gifts: take these clothes for the road.

Who hasn't seen deer lying dead on the highway, shattered and broken, guts ballooning out, limbs askew, blood staining the ears and nose? Who's missed the mess in the ditch later on, once the maggots and beetles move in? This was his marriage, in short. Or it was then, anyway, with him half-dead in the chill at the window, stripped to his briefs, inspecting his moonlit up-to-code porch. He kept thinking he heard her outside. Blond Kim treading up from the road.

Just before daylight, he snapped on the lamp. He checked Cindy's belongings again, the jewelry box on the dresser and the expensive perfumes. He stared and assessed—so many dresses and skirts—uncertain how long each empty hanger had hung empty. Finally he picked the phone up and dialed the sheriff.

The dispatcher asked was this an emergency. He told her his house had been robbed. He told her who did it.

What was stolen? the dispatcher asked.

Clothes, he said—feeling his house, and more of his world, his life, slide away. Then he noticed the mini-recorder by the lamp on the table. The dispatcher had put him on hold. He picked the recorder up and rewound it a click, thinking here's where the girl left her message, where she'll say she'll be back in a day. He listened.

Just his own unhappy voice and the sound of his engine. Another unwritable memo to Cindy.

I am not a nice man, the voice said on the tape. But I've tried, and will still try, to be good.

The dispatcher asked was he willing to sign and press charges. Don started to shiver. The nuns and monks were still humming, exhaling ancient empty tunes of the East. He felt he'd awakened after two months of sleep. It was like he just woke shocked to discover that winter had changed into spring. Soon the woodstove wouldn't need to be filled. The river'd turn clear, flow low in its channel. Woodpeckers would thump. Fish would bite and get caught.

Are you there? the dispatcher asked.

He was. For one frozen second in that cracking and sinking, that pause between pauses, he was.

Still Life with Candles
and Spanish Guitar

The story goes roughly like this: girl meets boy in chat room, agrees to meet downtown for coffee. And does, and after three minutes of coffee can see it's not good. The story goes like such stories do. Girl's got to ditch boy but can't simply snub him outright; he's not for her, but he's human and not stupid, either. What's more, he isn't ugly, has what you'd call middling good looks, with a kind of weird dark charisma, despite the clothes: he spent eighteen months in the army, was discharged for ambiguous reasons, and still wears mainly khaki. So girl suffers the droning self-centered barrage and says well, okay, yes, she'll join him for dinner, and get this, hops in his *minivan* in the freezing parking garage (boy has no children, no trade, not even a job), leaving her own car there on level three, trusting the universe to protect her, as it must, asking herself why in God's name she does these things that she does.

Lucky for her and for us, the story doesn't end in this vein. Boy does not pull off into a dimly lit lane to rape her and cut her with his knife and burn her and maybe cannibalize her a bit for good measure. Girl does not become a statistic, another in a long list of sorry bodies that turn up piecemeal in dumpsters. This is a happier story, unhappy as both girl and boy seem to be. First he sideswipes a wall, descending the parking garage. Turns out the van is his mother's, he borrowed it and, in fact, rarely drives (this in part was the rub with the army), though he's just turned thirty-three. With forced nonchalance, he pilots the damaged van to the valet lot at Atherton's, the city's most illustrious eatery, and in they go. Into the tableau of Italian suits, diamonds, candles, magnificent dresses—to the dismay of said girl, clad humbly in Levis and tennies and a white poly-knit top. The boy has brought his guitar in its uncomely case. They like me to play here, he told her outside. Anytime. Really.

The bar upstairs is a degree or two less formal, if not quite your jeans or khakis locale. And it's brimming with murmuring December tipplers. Boy squeezes through with his instrument, followed by girl; they claim the single unoccupied table, a tiny walnut thing trimmed in brushed chrome, like the bar. He unsheathes the guitar, tunes briefly. The girl motions as the waitperson passes, but he's looking every direction but theirs. The boy kicks off his set at the table with a burst of flamenco. The murmur halts in the bar for a moment as this new element registers. This Spanish brashness so forwardly flung, unprompted, so at odds with the holiday music. With "God Rest Ye," issuing still through the invisible speakers.

The boy retunes between songs. He hadn't gotten the guitar tuned in the first place. He doesn't get it right now. He's tone deaf, or nervous, or both; he's only been playing eight months. The waiter glides over at last, addressing them—boy, girl, guitar—as if from some immeasurable distance. Beer for the boy, scotch on the rocks for the girl. And an order of fries and steamed clams, since the boy said there'd be dinner. Boy blasts off again. Another fervent song by Montoya. It's all flamenco, actually. Flamenco's what the boy knows, it's his passion, his love. That and playing in public. Which he does with much flair: head jerks, grimaces, dramatic down strums.

Two songs later, the girl slips away to the bathroom. She opens her purse on the spotless mica-flecked marble counter, extracts her cell phone and dials her housemate. Sharon, she'll say when said housemate picks up, I blew it, come rescue me *now*—no, better yet, invent an emergency, something terrible, just call my cell in ten minutes. But Sharon's not home. Girl leaves message on voice mail, conveying just a fraction of the desperation she feels, then enters a stall, latching the elegant latch on the veined marble door, and unzipping, sits. She doesn't have to pee, but, well, here she is.

She's gone out of her way lately finding these least feasible men. Tonight seems to epitomize all, the whole sad vivid tally. There was the bewildered professor, a guitar player also, who didn't and would never know what he wanted, who couldn't say what he meant for all his fondness for words and was, by the way, married. There was the brother of her ex-roommate Stella, psychotic, volcanic, a bona fide stalker after the fact. There was the computer astronomer, whose very face made one want to yawn, and Seth, who was addicted to pot; there was the lovable drug and alcohol counselor with his less lovable herpes. And yes, the man who comanaged the greeting card factory, too old for her, really, who couldn't be pleased unless she played boy to his girl, unless she forcefully "took" him; and she *likes* being a girl, and feels strange, not sexy, with plastic accoutrements strapped to her hips.

For sure, one can be forgiven for doing what one does again and again and again. Girl meets boy after boy after worst possible boy. But what hurts is knowing you do it, and knowing you know, and knowing you haven't learned. What hurts is playing the role willingly, knowing in your bones how dire the ending will be. Even in the oldest, most basic stories, the wolf hides its teeth badly. And the girl knows what a wolf is, and knows about teeth, and still dares the thing to bare its teeth fully.

She sits biding her minutes, jeans at her ankles. Then gets up and zips up and checks herself in the mirror and then exits. She passes the Christmas ficus with its tiny white bulbs, the row of gleaming barstools, the cheerful holiday couples; she settles again at the table, where the boy is playing full tilt. Bar goers glance over occasionally. A few look embarrassed. Above all they don't know how to respond. *Why are these people here?* they seem to wonder, this smiling pretty girl with the mole and all her white teeth and this manic young man in black boots and khakis. They don't see a bowl or a tip jar. Will the girl walk around in a while with a hat, a sombrero? And the boy might choose, if he would, to play a bit softer.

One more clam, she decides, one last sip of scotch, and she'll say she's got to go. She's feeling sick, she will say, it's her stomach, the seafood perhaps; she hasn't had a clam since she was seven. She looks at the antique leaded windows, which are just slightly steamy, then at the bar, squinching her face up, trying to will her guts to rebel. That's when she sees the woman. A short erect little lady, mid-seventies, maybe, clad in cobalt chenille. The lady's not drinking, nor is she with anyone. She's just standing there gazing. At the girl, at the boy—three paces off, serenely smiling.

The boy ends his song with a flourish. The woman applauds emphatically, edging up, inciting the first general applause of the evening.

Wonderful, she says, beaming.

Her face is exuberant, radiant, rosy. The house music intones from on high, cautiously operatic. *And heaven and nature sing, and heaven and nature sing!*

Thanks, says the boy.

The woman beams at the girl, the boy, the guitar. Do you know "The Hunt" by Albéniz? she asks.

Still working on that one, the boy answers.

Marvelous.

Thanks, says the boy.

Are you here every Saturday? We're downstairs. I never come up here.

I just come around when I can.

I see, the woman says.

She's swaying minutely, touching the girl's chair to keep herself steady.

Would you play for us? she asks the boy. At my table? Down-stairs?

The boy looks at the girl.

Just two songs, the woman says. We'll pay you.

The girl's got her hand on her gut, face squinched, but doesn't speak up in time.

Okay, says the boy, and stands up. And the girl says, I'll wait here, and the woman says, Oh honey, no, he's playing for *you!*

Downstairs it's a soft-spoken party of six. White linen, candles, maroon linen napkins. At the table's head a pair of diners slide over, making space for the girl and the boy and the acoustic guitar. The woman's husband, who resembles Marcus Welby, MD, orders a beer for the boy and a scotch for the girl, looking half-vexed but too gracious to ask his dear wife, What have you gone and done now. The boy tunes, then rolls into the Montoya piece he opened with earlier. This time he gets every note right, the song is flawless, mi-nus a few rhythmic stumbles. He concludes, panting almost. The whole table applauds. As do others; other tables, other diners, who seem at least vaguely interested in what is transpiring at this end of the room. The piped-in Christmas carols have been summarily si-lenced. The waiter hands the desserts around, coffee. The boy rolls into song two.

The woman seems entranced by the girl. She's beaming and beaming, confiding, utterly wrong but somehow also right in her way, her fine silver hair swept in a bun, gazing over the bouquet of hibiscus and holly, the candles, the neck of the Spanish guitar. The boy moves into song three, and then four. There's no stop-ping him now, he might play forever, and that's fine with her, with the woman, even if her party's begun again to converse, and the old man on her left, liver spots, baggy red velvet vest, half-blind and half-deaf and maybe touched by Tourette's, is nodding off slowly.

This is how it feels to be young and in love, her face seems to say. This is how we're made love to, this is how love comes at us deliciously headlong. This is how we flower and live in it because it's all that matters, ever. I know this well, her face seems to say.

And I refuse to forget it, or lose it. And I know you'll remember it, too.

And now the girl's phone is going off, it's clipped to her hip, not ringing but vibrating in its imperative way. And in this happier unhappy story of girl and boy, this story that could and does go on without end, the girl lets it buzz. She melts into her chair and her scotch and stays where she is.

Salvage

Pruitt knew damned well what he had bought. But he'd always been a sucker for good deals and couldn't resist this one, no way, not with government agencies involved and foreclosure and desperation selling. A big part of his job, he'd told himself in the past, was cashing in on people's catastrophes.

He shook another lemon drop out of the bag and stuck it in his mouth, keeping the accelerator pinned to the floor as he took the hill. He sucked the candy and watched in the big rectangle of mirror as John, beginning his own ascent a quarter of a mile back, fell behind.

Piece of shit truck, he said, alone in the cab.

Pruitt had owned the trucks a dozen years now. He had a third one at home in the yard a year older than these—out of commission—along with a loader, some detachable buckets. He'd have to get John's truck back into the shop soon, he knew. It was sounding sicker all the time. But with the profit he'd be making on this mountain of corn, it would be no problem. He broke the lemon drop between his teeth. No problem at all.

At Buttonwillow, he crossed Interstate 5 and lumbered north to Shafter, John right behind him. They hit Highway 99 south of Famoso and, unimpeded now by hills, began to pick up speed.

The corn was grown by a man living out west of McKittrick, a man who had dreams about getting himself into political office. He'd re-mortgaged his farm and everything, Pruitt had heard, to help support that conspiracy nut, what's-his-name, who ran for the presidency a few years back. Eventually the creditors moved in, came after this farmer, and seized not only his house and silo and tractors but his crops as well, including a mound of corn he'd rushed to harvest in a race against the bill-collectors.

LaRouche. The idiot's name.

The corn had too much moisture in it from the start, it couldn't be stored safely. It'd been mishandled. Pruitt would handle it from here. This was their first trip down and back, two more to go.

He pulled the truck off the highway at Selma, signaling to John. They disembarked at a coffee shop near the freeway, left the trucks idling in the parking lot.

Some pretty stinky corn we got, Mr. Pruitt, John said, putting his cheeseburger down and pointing out the window with his thumb. Don't think we ever hauled anything looked this bad before.

Eat your lunch, Pruitt said. When I want your ideas I'll ask.

Fine, John said, watching the waitress, who leaned forward in her polyester skirt, filling coffee cups in another booth.

Fresh out of high school, John had worked for Pruitt since Phillip quit. John was better at dealing with his boss's moods than Phillip, who started driving the trucks when Pruitt's son, Dennis, had finally had enough of his dad's business, and of his dad, and moved away to college.

Pruitt poured the rest of his Coke over the ice, stirring it around with the straw. What do you know about animal feed? he asked, his voice less sarcastic now. You're not eating the stuff, are you? You planning to become a cow?

John pulled at his fingers with his napkin and said, I ain't no cow, don't plan to be.

Pruitt gazed out the window. Beyond the parking lot the wind brought the dust up in swirls, blowing the occasional mini-tornado in the dry field beside the road. The highway marker faced them, white letters on dusty green. It read: REEDLEY, 12, OROSI, 31.

The first and maybe the last woman Pruitt ever loved was from around here, raised over near Reedley. He'd met her one night at a square dance in Fresno, and the next night she came home with him. She was skinny, sure, but she had these huge green eyes, and she laughed at his jokes, and made love like a demon. Anne, her name was—Jesus God, talk about magic. She made all the other women he'd ever been with in his life, all two, seem like nothing. She even made him stop thinking about himself for a while.

She lived in Virginia now, the length of a continent away, with her husband and kid. Or that was the last Pruitt knew; he hadn't heard anything in eighteen years. It wasn't that he didn't love his wife. He did, naturally. But not the way he'd loved this girl from Reedley. No, he'd never felt that, never would again. By the time Pruitt got married he'd given up trying to find duplicates for that other time. That other girl.

Pruitt fixed his eyes on John's pimpled face. A cow don't care what it eats, he told him. We mix this stuff in with the other grain, the untainted stuff, like we always do. Cow's got a tough stomach.

Sure, boss.

Wipe that smile off your face, dingleberry.

Sure, boss, John said.

———————

Before his son left for college, things got pretty ugly around the house. Dennis was staying out all night with friends, smoking pot, drinking, staggering home hours after the birds started to chirp. Once he came home sailing on something, LSD or whatever. Pruitt heard him from his bed, caught him banging into things downstairs with a wide-eyed, wacko look on his face, too stoned to speak.

Mornings, he'd be so tired, so dead, he couldn't help Pruitt with the loader even, or hop in the truck to make a delivery.

Pruitt would knock him around at times. It would get ugly. He'd threaten him, ground him. Nothing seemed to work.

He's just at that age, Pruitt's wife would say.

That age nothing, Lorraine, Pruitt would answer. The kid's pissing on us. Poisoning himself, throwing money away. Money he needs to be saving.

But that was then. Nine months ago he'd gone off to Modesto to live in the dorm. He hadn't been back since he moved, even though it was midsummer now. He hardly ever called. Things were calmer with Dennis gone, no doubt about that. John worked for Pruitt full-time, worked hard and did what he was told. No bellyaching. No headaches at all.

We'll unload there near the shed, Pruitt said.

He swung the rig around the yard, raising a cloud of dust. His wife had come out on the porch, as usual, to watch. She took her apron off and shook it, leaning over the wooden rail.

Don't you maybe want to dump this farther away from the house, Mr. Pruitt? John asked, sounding fake-nonchalant. He spat, pushing dirt over the wet place on the ground with his toe.

Pruitt hit the compression release and dropped down from the cab, grunting.

Don't you maybe want to mind your own business, son? What's it to you, anyway, shit hook?

Ain't nothing to me, John said, smirking almost, turning back to his truck.

Pruitt's wife called out from the porch. Pruitt, she said.

Hang on, Pruitt called back.

———

He wasn't surprised, he told his wife.

She'd gotten a call from the Stanislaus county jail, Dennis asking if they could come up and post his bail. It was only a matter of time, he told his wife, what with the trouble the boy'd always gotten into with the neighbors and at school. It was only logical he'd land himself in jail.

The kid could just stay in there another night, Pruitt decided. Let him think about his stupidity—drunkenness in public, destruction of property, resisting arrest, whatever else he was in for. Besides, Pruitt thought, pushing away from the dinner table, gut swelling out even more than usual, he himself was fifty-one years old, shit, and he'd been driving since seven in the morning. He'd be damned if was going to drive some more.

He moved to the porch while his wife cleaned up. He sank down in the overstuffed chair, too tired to look for the newspaper or reach for the light. Two pieces of pie was overdoing it, he supposed. But goddamn that kid.

The wind had knocked off pretty much—it usually did this time of the evening. There wasn't a moon, but Pruitt could still see the shapes of the trucks hulking side-by-side in the dark. Beside the black shape of the shed was the black shape of the corn, his grain-mountain, glowing faintly with the fungus that was eating it up.

He'd have to get on this one in a hurry, grind it and mix it up and ship it the hell out fast. Even an eighteen-year-old kid, Pruitt thought, can see this is nothing to mess with.

———————————

Dennis's apartment was cleaner than Pruitt thought it would be, maybe because Dennis didn't own enough of anything to clutter it up, nothing but a bicycle and a sleeping bag and whatever, some books. While the boy was in the shower Pruitt snooped around the place a little. This place he'd been paying for in part, the student loans covering the rest.

In the bedroom was a thirty-gallon aquarium resting on a plastic milk crate by the window. Pruitt kneeled down. The thing was full of dry sand and cactuses and jagged rocks, home to the ugliest-looking creatures Pruitt had ever laid eyes on. Scorpions, but five times bigger than any scorpion he'd ever seen. The nasty armor-plate bodies shone black, yellow, and blue, lit by the overhead light-bulb. One backed up a little, raising its claws.

By the boy's sleeping bag was a battered desk lamp, resting on another plastic crate. Inside the crate were some novels, science fiction mostly, and a notebook with a pen clipped on the front. Dennis had been writing to himself, Pruitt saw, not letters to people or assignments for teachers, just lots of rambling, most of it about some girl, probably the one he moaned about earlier. He stuck the notebook back where he found it and went to see what Dennis had in the refrigerator.

He tried to be nice, like his wife said he should be, once his son had cleaned up and dressed. He'd called the boy dumbfuck and peckerhead and shit-for-brains in the car coming back from the jail. There wasn't much left he could call him, and he was tired of being pissed off. So he told Dennis about developments in the business, and about John. He leaned over the Formica counter while his son made coffee, describing the great deal he'd gotten, this monster pile of corn.

She fucked me over, Dad, Dennis said.

Watch your mouth, boy, Pruitt said.

She made me think she liked me, then started with somebody else, Dennis said. It drives me bat shit thinking about it.

They drank instant coffee out of plastic cups. Pruitt wished there was milk to put in his. Don't think, then, he said. It won't help things any.

I can't help it, Dad. I can't stop thinking.

Feeling sorry, Pruitt came close to telling Dennis about the time his own life caved in on him. This was when he was twenty-two, living in Fresno, the time Anne from Reedley floored him with her abrupt change of heart, her explanations, her new boyfriend. He wanted to tell Dennis how the whole rest of his life had been tainted by this one bad scene; since then nothing ever turned out like he'd hoped. But he thought again. These are not the kinds of things you tell your son.

You mess with women, Denny, he said instead, you're going to get stung. Take it from me.

He turned away. Dennis had gotten skinnier since Christmas. His hair was long now, almost to his shoulders. The cops or somebody had knocked hell out of him, too, bruising one side of his face, swelling up his lip. The shower'd helped a little, but not much.

You look like shit, son, Pruitt said.

———————

Late in the week, a man in a county inspector's pickup appeared at Pruitt's place, and, as John told Pruitt later, wrenched out a little piece of the corn-pile with some tongs. He stuffed the corn in a bottle, John said, and took it away.

Two days after that this same inspector returned with another one—a man in a state-owned car. They stood a long time in front of the corn-mound, which was twelve feet high and seventy feet long, though keeping their distance, marking things down on their clipboards.

They finally asked Pruitt, who was there to meet them the second time, what the hell he thought he was doing.

Goddamn motherfucker shit, Pruitt yelled after they'd gone, yelling at no one in particular. Son of a holy motherfucking bitch!

Pruitt, his wife said, gliding up.

Get out, he said, leaning over the sink, wondering whether or not he'd be sick.

That pile had cost him nearly ten thousand dollars, and they were telling him he couldn't touch it. He'd have to wait, they said, until they decided what to do. Pruitt was sure he'd been set up, turned into somebody's jackass.

Ed, his wife said, putting her hand on his back, lightly. Tell me.

He opened the door of the refrigerator, snatched a couple of beers out, then fumed into the living room, crashed onto the couch. His wife crept along behind. He finished the first beer in two gulps. He opened the other one, then slid over on the couch to let Lorraine sit down.

Son of a fucking bitch, he said, quieter now.

He hunched forward over his belly, turning the beer can around, denting the cold aluminum with his thumbs.

Ed, what, Lorraine asked.

Pruitt looked at his hands, saw them shake in a way he couldn't control. His wife took the can away from him and set it on the coffee table.

In their first years of marriage, Lorraine would kneel over him and let her hair swing, sweeping it softly back and forth over his face and naked chest and belly. In later years she'd cut her hair. Then she'd gotten fat, fat as her Mexican mother. She snored now, loud as he did.

Lorraine, he said, they're going to ruin me.

How? she said, her voice consoling. How?

Pruitt told her how. He finished his beer, and told her. He told her how he'd not only lose his investment but have to pay to have the stuff carted off, disposed of in any way they saw fit. Sixty thousand or more it could cost, seeing how, as the inspector said, this was the most poisonous grain they'd ever tested. So much for fixing the trucks. Or putting a new roof on the shed.

In an odd way, though, Pruitt felt relieved. These last years he'd been feeling weird about his work, not that he'd admit it to anybody. He'd read articles. Aflatoxin—the fungus out there making his corn light up—did strange things to the food chain, he learned. He read about children drinking contaminated milk, about brain defects, about infected mothers bearing babies with flippers instead of arms. He'd read, understood, felt bad for a while, then carried on with his job.

If he didn't do it, somebody else would.

He didn't drink much milk. He was careful where he bought when he did, knowing the dairies by heart and who bought what from whom.

Maybe he'd have to just pack it all in, retire early. Maybe he'd have to go on welfare or whatever, live off the government like his son.

Whatever happens happens, Pruitt, his wife said. We'll be okay. She pushed at the tight spots on his neck with her fingers. Bad things happen, they do. And then it gets better.

The great removal took place six weeks later, at midnight, after the wind had died down. The removal specialists told him he'd have to keep himself and his family inside, so Pruitt watched from the window, watched as trucks lined up in the bright moonlight for loading.

The toxic waste team wore thick yellow suits and yellow bubble helmets, looking to Pruitt for all the world like astronauts. Oxygen tanks hung from their backs, hoses snaking over their shoulders. Men from the volunteer fire department stood at a distance with goggles on, bandannas hiding their noses and mouths, dousing the pile with a jet of water whenever corn-dust started to fly. Pruitt saw John out there with them, he being a volunteer fireman and all, not to mention a curious shitting little twerp. Beyond the line of trucks a van hunkered, television call letters printed on the side. A man squatted on top, swiveling a movie camera around; then the camera's eye zeroed in on Pruitt's house.

Shit, Pruitt said, moving away from the window.

Lorraine came into the living room to check on Dennis. She kept him in shorts now, a plastic mat underneath him at all times. Since he'd been to the hospital he didn't know enough to get up and go to the bathroom.

They got a goddamned movie camera out there, Pruitt told his wife. My corn's on TV.

Lorraine leaned the boy back in his chair, fussing with his hair. They've seen worse things than this, she said, on TV.

Christ, Pruitt said, trying not to look at his son.

Valley Hospital in Modesto called a month ago, saying Dennis had arrived by ambulance and was in emergency care. Considering the variety and quantity of the drugs in him, the police called it attempted suicide, though nobody'd found a note. He'd come out of the coma all right, but where he ended up, Pruitt thought, wasn't a whole lot better, or different. The kid's arms hung limp at his sides. His mouth was open all the time. He didn't know his father from President Reagan.

After they brought him home, Pruitt drove to Modesto to clean the apartment. He vacuumed and mopped and washed windows, got the security deposit back from the landlady, paid the overdue rent. He put the boy's bicycle in the back of the pickup, along with his bedding and clothes and books and other odds and ends, pictures of the girl. Pruitt had to go to three different pet shops trying to get rid of the scorpions. When he finally found somebody to take them he didn't care about money, money for the spiders or for the tank. He gave the whole goddamned mess away.

Driving south, he felt so tired and sick and pissed he thought his head would explode. He wondered if the girl knew what Dennis had done. She was to blame in this, if anybody was. He'd wanted to take her by the shoulders and shake her, the bitch. See? he'd say. *See?* Look what you did!

Driving south past Turlock toward Merced and Chowchilla, Pruitt got so mad he had to pull off the road, honking the horn and beating the dashboard.

He was so mad he was crying, he hardly knew where he was.

The sound of the loader outside made the windows rattle. They'd brought a big one in, brand-new county equipment, school bus yellow, fresh new tires. Pruitt sat down by the window, a glass of bourbon in his hand.

A man in a spacesuit sat in the loader, topping off a truck with a last bucketful of corn. The moon lit his suit up, beamed off the surface of his plastic facepiece. As the loader arm pivoted away, four more men in helmets scaled the sides of the truck. They pulled a tarp over the load, tucking it into plastic sleeves lining the bed.

They poured epoxy over the seams, sealing the whole thing up the way Lorraine Ziploced squash and cucumbers and turnips in the fall to stash in the freezer for later.

This was the fourth truck. Pruitt had been counting. They'd be at this all night, or almost.

Lorraine, Pruitt said to his wife, why don't you put him to bed now.

Lorraine glanced at Pruitt from the couch, looked back at the magazine she was reading.

Well, I guess, she said.

Why don't you go to bed now, too?

She stood, stepped across to gaze out the window beside him. I guess I will.

John and somebody else walked by the porch carrying a fire hose, both keeping their distance from the loader, the operation in progress. John glanced at the window in passing and made as if to wave, but nodded instead. Pruitt shook his head.

Dickbrain, he said. And then: Lorraine, go to bed.

He scuffed over to the couch and lay down. He sat up in a minute, unlaced his boots and took them off. Then he reached across and pulled a few books out of Dennis's bag and lay back. Textbooks, they were—*Agricultural Biology* and *Essentials of Agribusiness.* Not very interesting, really, but Pruitt had skimmed them before and thought they looked worth his while. He might be changing his profession soon, for all he knew; Christ, an old man like him. A man with an established, respectable business. A man who nobody in their right mind would buy grain from again. Not around here, anyway.

He'd already read from the thick book, the biology book, about *Aspergillus flavus,* the fungus that kept him and his family alive all these years. A name like a Roman goddamned king, he thought. Behold the Emperor of Shit. He didn't care to read any more about that, or to eat peanut butter again, either. If most people knew what grew on the skins of peanuts, they'd think twice, too.

After a while, he fell asleep. He'd come out of his doze every so often, hear the windows shudder or the loader arm scrape against the steel back end of a truck, and then sleep some more. He left the lights on and burning, all of them.

Just before daybreak, he groaned and sat up. He closed the book and, scooping up the other one, reached for the bag. As he shoved the books back he saw the notebook he'd peeked at Dennis's that day. He pulled it out. COMP BOOK, the letters read across the front. And in the lined area at the bottom, written in pen, DENNIS PRUITT.

He'd read the notebook over more carefully since the mishap, looking for answers, wondering if there was anything in there about him. He hadn't gone over every page, though. He opened it now and started flipping through, fuzzy-eyed. He found a place he didn't remember, and read:

I got my second scorpion today. A Peruvian Yellow-Tail, to be exact, a big fucker with a brown body and yellow claws and a yellow stinger in his tail. The other one, the blue one, doesn't mind him so I don't think they'll fight. They could have killed each other but no. I like seeing them walk around on the sand, they seem happy in there crawling around. My neighbor Kyle came in a while ago, snuck in on me without knocking and saw me staring at my scorpions. He looked at me like I was a stupid fuck or something. But I don't care what he thinks, or what Molly or anybody thinks, because they are mine. And I have more on order.

Pruitt closed the notebook and got up, pinching at the cramp in his neck. He walked to the door and went out on the porch.

The last of the trucks had left an hour ago, bound for Casmalia, no doubt, final resting place for unkillable poisons. Early sun lit the foothills beyond Tollhouse to the east. In the dimness Pruitt saw the hole they'd scraped in his yard, the gouge they made wanting to get it all. He walked down the wooden steps into the dirt. He could give a fuck about socks.

He stopped to stare at the scar in his yard. Torn earth; wet muddy rocks wrenched into light. He stood staring, thinking. What would John do now, the poor dildo? Nobody'd hire that ugly wiseass sack of shit. He'd end up in a burger pit, working with Mexicans. Pruitt stared at the place where his corn used to be, this corn he'd paid a fortune for and would pay to have carted away. The wind rose again, blowing the dust around.

Motherfuckers, he said, climbing into his truck.

He snapped on the ignition and watched the starter glow, then fired the engine, pumping the accelerator, dust and pebbles sticking to his sock.

This thing would end up in court, he knew, but who knew how it all would turn out. They could always start over, move to a different state. Or he could just drive this piece of shit into the shed and close the door behind him. He hadn't handled things so well lately, he'd be the first to admit it. There was only so much he could take.

He rammed in the clutch and shoved the thing in gear. These were his trucks. He'd drive each and every one into the river before they could take these babies away.

Be with Somebody

I went anyway. I went to Club Mecca, tipsy already, and drank. I
moved table to table, afraid of what and who I might see, then hung
at the door, torn between staying and leaving, breathing smog in
rather than smoke. Cars hissed like surf on the boulevard, clubbers
and perverts slid up the sidewalk. Above, beyond the traffic and
ramshackle furniture store, Mr. M shot his squint at the city—M as
in Marlboro—crow's feet, receding hairline, the meadow behind
blinding, glaring its electric-green beauty. I leaned in the doorway,
fading, and said to myself, David, you miserable faggot, go home,
the longer you stay the more stupid you'll feel, the more sick you'll
be in the morning. Then a woman was swaying beside me, claiming
the opposite doorjamb—woman, I say, but girl is more like it. She
looked barely twenty in her black lamé jumpsuit and white thigh-
highs, breasts leaping out at the front.

God, she said, not looking over.

God what? I asked, wanting to run.

Just plain God, she said, sighing. She dug around in her purse, which sparkled, made with leftover cloth, no doubt, from her suit. Her arms and cleavage glowed pale red, thanks to taillights and maybe strong liquor. Her perm seemed uneven—she might have had it done in Wyoming. A pair of people pushed between us, down the three steps to the sidewalk.

I can't believe this, she said, digging.

You left your IQ at home?

She snapped her purse shut, smiling, and glanced at my crotch. She said she forgot her inhaler, which she used for her asthma. Should keep a spare on her person, I told her. Where, she said; I raised my eyebrows. Engines hummed. A honk. The DJ rattled inside over the pulsating techno, too garbled to hear. One more minute and I'd be gone, up the block to Brentano, the parking lot, my beckoning car.

Well, what's your excuse? she asked. I came out to breathe.

I'm hiding, I said.

She's inside?

She got it half-right; I left it at that. I felt as old as I was—twice her age, surely. Clubbers pressed out the door. A woman stepped up to come in. Aquamarine shorts, white belt, white pumps, top patterned in gold and black zebra. Her expression said she thought we were bouncers.

ID please, I said.

She pulled a driver's license out. Heather Mitcheltree, it read. She lived in Arcadia, if the thing wasn't fake. I tilted the card toward the streetlight, scrutinizing, or pretending to.

That's five dollars, my partner said, as I handed the card back. Miss Mitcheltree pulled a five from her pocket. I was about to object but the acting was good, why spoil it? Thanks, said my partner—adding the bill to bills she already had in her hand—have a good night.

You're bad, I said, after the woman stepped in.

Why?

Bad, bad, I said, and grabbed the five and walked in to give it back to the woman. But the woman was fast, one sand grain in the vibrating mob. I politely pushed through, seeking odd alleys in the human crush, bumbling first toward the tables in back then the veranda, past the genuine-simulated zinc bar and frantic bartenders and flapping laughing dressed-to-the-hilt clubbers, up to the stage, over which the word MECCA appeared, smoky, in pseudo-deco pink neon, and pendulant death-pale papier-mâché people-things rotated and swung. Everybody was here, everybody was dancing. The music deafened. So much postindustrial noise, far from the disco we the once-innocent loved.

Anybody who'd been here knew there was no cover weekdays. Tomorrow, yes, when Strikemaster would play, and Saturday too, when the true gay crowd arrived and Black Fag took the stage, with their demi-dada performance-art punk, featuring six-foot three-inch drag queen of color, Vaginal Creme Davis. But Heather M. didn't know. I nudged through the roar to redeem her, her now-sweaty five dollar bill in my hand. Then I saw Perry, as I knew I would have to. The old kick in the stomach again. Frozen, I hung by a fake Roman column, spying on him and the Man from Steroid, this guy he'd been seeing. They sat on the balcony, a dozen tall empty drinks on their table, hunched forward, tendering words the way one did here, half an inch from the ear, aided by sign language. I felt ill, drinking it in. Perry's black hair hanging in ringlets, the sloping shoulders, precious arch in his back; the way he cocked his head before speaking. His forehead and nose, the indefatigable chin. And this Neanderthal half-wit who got to enjoy it; I'd met him, with his slutty demeanor, all the intellectual depth of a slug. I looked and assessed, hoisting my petard a notch or two higher, got jostled, dropped the five bucks, bent down to snatch it and got bumped on the head, almost threw up.

A couple stood in the vestibule, tattooed and pierced, old punkers. The man was putting his wallet away.

You pay cover? I asked him. Yeah, he said, touching the hairy back of his hand—she didn't stamp me. Here, I said, no cover tonight, giving him Heather's five and five more from my billfold.

She charged us ten each, he said.

I sighed, gave him ten more.

The girl sat on the step, head wagging over her apocalyptic breasts, fat wad of bills in her fist. I wondered how much she'd made in eight or ten minutes. One of her white tights, I noticed, was smudged.

You're terrible, I said.

Her eyes seemed puffier now, her face more flushed. She wheezed, gripping the marsupial pouch of her purse on her belly, sounding like an antique bellows, or something drying up in a tide pool. She needed a doctor, for all I knew, but was too drunk and too sick of her lot on this planet to care.

At the all-night acres-wide drugstore I sat in the car, waiting while she, Gwendolyn, went to buy her inhaler. I'd nosed my hood in against the front windows, there under the fluorescent-bright signs for sale-priced diapers, tissues, shavers, make-up, portable barbecues. I sat, hands in lap, seat half-reclined, half-listening to *Loveline*, a late-night call-in where teenagers confessed to a wiseacre host and a doctor, seeking advice. Without effort I could have stuck a disc in, but didn't, too alcohol-stupid to move. Traffic blurred along behind me, on Turnby. My engine ticked, anxious for the 605 East, and suburbs, silence, my tidy garage.

She was raised near Lake Erie, northwest Pennsylvania, in a town, she'd said, where nobody young stuck around. Where you froze nine months of the year and boiled for three, and wine cost a fortune; where men showed up at their weddings with toothpicks in mouth, and a twelve-pack and bug zapper were prime entertainment. She started college in Cleveland, dropped out, moved all the way west to this city, enrolled and dropped out again. She'd go to law school, she said, if she could; I told her it figured. She'd lied to her folks about school this term and they called up and checked and cut her off. She'd tried working, that was okay, but she wouldn't take just anything, i.e., a guttersnipe job. No fast food or phone sales. No pizza delivery.

A boy's voice leaked from the speakers. I like these girls with big muscles, he stuttered, ashamed.

And you think that makes you a homo, said the wiseacre host.

Riki, shut up, the doctor said.

What's taking this girl? I wondered, turning the radio up. She might be shoplifting, it occurred to me. Would I get popped as an accessory? At any rate, I'd be driving her home. She shared a West Side apartment, evidently. Somebody had dropped her off at Mecca, and the friend she'd expected, a man she supposedly trusted, had burned her, failed to show.

A car pulled in beside mine on the left and a man and woman got out. The man bearded, baseball cap, protuberant gut. The woman, protuberant also, wore shorts, thongs, a blue T-shirt that said Shut Up and Do Me. As they lumbered past on the walkway, the woman paused, eyeing my car, called to her husband, said something inaudible, nodded, bent down, checked out my fender, straightened, said something else, then retraced her steps and stopped at my window; as the glass lowered, she smiled.

What kind of car is this, mind if I ask?

I told her.

You're normal, said Riki, the radio host.

I told you, the woman said to her husband. You owe me. She bounced on the balls of her feet, jiggling. Then unhasped the purse on her shoulder and pulled a card out and slipped it to me— *Paradise Auto Body*, it read, blue and black on off-white. John and Jean Crump, proprietors. She eyed my car again, the side panels and trunk, with something like lust. Stop in if you crash it, she said.

I clicked the dome light on when they'd gone, glanced at my face in the mirror.

Late evenings and mornings were worst. A thin pale Mr. M is how I appeared in this light, with less hair and nothing noble to squint at. Of course I'd prepared myself in advance, telling the world I was forty on my thirty-eighth birthday, to hear it exclaim how youthful, how boyish, I looked. Like Gwendolyn, I seemed young for my age. But Perry's defection had whacked a spike in my guts, wilting me utterly. I stared out the windshield. Concrete and litter, and on the storefront, Day-Glo green and pink signs. Pampers, one hundred count, four-forty-nine.

This was what I got for hunting pups. Perry, I mean, and the sweetmeats before him. I knew better. You had to feel like a fogy confronted with that. With energy, intensity, beauty, all a slap in face to the fact that dreams go to seed. *Perry!* He reminded me of *me* at his age, which is to say twenty-three. Dancing all night any night of the week, and day after day at the beach, no sunscreen, no visor, just you and a friend on a double-wide towel, breeze lovingly grazing your skin. If someone got hurt it was his risk, not yours, unsaid or not. Now I knew how it felt, what I had done. I was downing glass after glass of what I had poured.

The girl bustled up, opened the door, and got in. The device was out of the package already. It hissed as she sucked at the gas.

Better?

Mucho, she said. She dropped the thing in the bag and pulled out some gum, sighing, administered a stick to herself, then offered me some. I declined.

Where can I take you? I asked, watching her watch herself wad up the wrapper. A little mascara-glob clung to one eyelash. Her lashes were long.

Wherever, she said.

Evidently her boyfriend, or should she say ex, would kill her if she returned to their place. Why? He owed her money, she said, and she, like, sold some of his stuff. A computer and microwave oven and things. I told her I had to go home. Let's go for coffee, she said. Breakfast. Smiling, rearing her cleavage, a kind of genuine-simulated seduction. She still couldn't see where my proclivities lay—I'm no fem, no male Scarlett O'Hara. For me the female body, with all due respect, is inviting as quicksand, the unfriendly swamp.

I work in the morning, I told her. It was true, I managed a

bookstore—I'd worked there forever, I didn't finish school either. Though I survived fairly comfortably, thanks to husbandry, frugality, my dead grandfolks' estate.

She'd consigned her worldly possessions, two bags and a box, to this man she trusted, she said; but if she went there, she knew, she'd wait at the door till four in the morning; he might not show up at all.

Gwen, I said—she'd didn't like *Gwendolyn*, clearly—I'm not sure I believe you.

Go for it, Riki said to a kid, a different kid, on the radio.

So far all I know, I said, is you're a liar and a thief.

This is the *truth*, she insisted. She leaned back in her seat, eyes closed, her face sort of folding in on itself. In a second, I figured, the tears would come. It sounds crazy, I know, she said, voice quavering. I mean, nothing like this ever happened before. I'm just trying, like, to know what to do.

Jean and John Crump shuffled past my bumper, plastic grocery bags dangling. John gripped a five-liter box of wine in one hand. They dropped the bags in the trunk and got in and backed up, Jean leveling one last long leer at my car. Meanwhile Gwendolyn talked, qualifying, explaining, backtracking, setting me straight as it were, with me feeling more ancient and useless as each minute ticked, lower than low on cheap scotch, sick to my corpuscles of living, of dwelling on Perry, and then indeed she was crying, sobbing, God, God what a mess, she'd just take the bus back to Mercer, or whatever her town was, and forget school, forget California, and marry some hick, some dildo fuck with a gun rack, and watch TV all day, cop out like everyone else did.

Okay, okay, I said, starting the car. You can stay on my couch.

Are you sure? she said, looking victorious, if a little afraid. I mean I've got enough for a motel, I guess, she said, and sniffed. She toked again on the inhaler. One of the jumpsuit straps had slipped down her shoulder.

We stopped at the stoplight at Highland and Eighth. The car beside us sported four cholos, heads uniformly shaved, lowered onto the seats, stereo blasting hip-hop, trunk thumping. With their uniform stares they checked Gwen out. She looked straight ahead.

It's like I just want to *be* with somebody, she said. Somebody smart like you, and sweet, and not broke, or a bum. Is that so much to ask?

What about law school, I thought. We rolled onto the freeway. After minutes of silence I asked her how she knew, in a strange car with a stranger, she wouldn't be murdered and raped and all that. Wasn't this risky? She said she thought I was cool, I couldn't be evil, so closely did I resemble her dad. She watched my face fall and added, Wait, no, I mean my dad's very handsome.

I'd gone home each day for three weeks dreading my house and unwinking message machine, so to be truthful a guest seemed in a way a welcome idea. A female, even. Anything but one of these one-night lays you find lurking at Mecca, aging faggots more pathetic even and desperate than me. I'd grown mean, I should say. I was snipping and biting at people even before Perry left—my family, my two or three friends, the kids at the bookstore. In my way I'd been mean to this woman Gwen. Who doesn't hate being a bitch? Having her here, I'd make up for things, take a night off from myself.

Now she slept in my bed. I said I'd take the couch. We'd talked until three, she under the covers in her jumpsuit and tights, me slouching at one edge of the mattress—on top of the covers—both of us sipping brandy I poured. I'd heard about her ex Chet or Chad and she'd heard about Perry, my depression, my father, the pills I finally quit taking, etc. She was brighter than I'd thought. She deserved more credit than I'd allotted; I'd been put off by the valley girl jargon. Sleep here with me, she said, conking out, meaning join her in bed. I was tempted. I had an antique for a couch, puritanically stern, like my dining room set. Besides, it would be nice not to sleep by myself. I didn't handle loneliness well.

I stripped down to my undies and clicked off the lamp, slipped in under the sheet. I tugged the blanket up on her shoulder—she lay on her side, facing my way. Her hair smelled of smoke, as mine did. She was wheezing, though softly. In dim light she looked like my sister, the nurse, who'd moved to Hawaii with her munchkin and army-man husband, a sister I didn't see anymore.

I'd hoped to get a degree in English or something. A master's or higher; I didn't even make my BA. I couldn't seem to finish anything then. At some point I settled for my boss's musty two acres of books, and there I remained. I liked reading. I liked being young, I liked seeing people light up with books. To be blunt, I got distracted by sex. I liked being noticed, I liked the excitement, up to my teeth in the intoxicant, love.

Perry was wrong from the start, I suppose. He'd appeared in the store requesting a title. I ordered the book and called when it arrived, and when he dropped in to get it, I issued it gratis. He thanked me, batting his lashes, 501s cradling his heavenly butt. I said we should talk, indicating the book, and he said, We are, and I said, Discuss, and he said, Discuss what? We wound up on my carpet, Chopin floating around us, then Debussy. It happened fast. I was wise and well-read to him. A father of sorts—a teacher, a guide, there to support and advise and maybe loan him money. I wore my camera out snapping his portrait, freezing the impossible present. In time he stopped calling. He stopped returning my calls. I fumed, I cried, got depressed and psychotic. Then he appeared on my step as if nothing had happened. He'd been busy, was all; he needed space. This happened twice. We started up as before and he did it again. I felt gutted, undone. I felt like a starfish, a starfish missing an arm, with another one stunted, severed but flowing again toward its Kirlian outline. I was ready to give up limb after limb, and befriend phantom pain, forgive and forgive and forgive, just to have him and love him again.

In bed beside me Gwendolyn moaned. She smacked her lips in her sleep, spoke. *I didn't*, she said, and turned over.

By now, though, I'd had it. Hadn't I? I would not call back if he called. I wouldn't set foot in Mecca, or Ambush, or Rage, or anywhere else he might be.

Moonlight streamed in the window, bleaching my great-grandmother's rocker, my grandfather's antique steamer trunk, the Edwardian dresser. In the tree by the window the mockingbird ran through its list of mimicking calls: mourning dove, starling, sparrow, and I swear it, the car-alarm sound. I'd heard this bird or its mate for a month now. It sustained my insomnia, and as I saw it, despair. Sleepless I'd lay while it mocked an emergency, and I'd hate Perry more, hate myself more, and hate my unforgiving, uncomprehending old father, who still thought I'd betrayed the whole family. I'd even hate Andrew, my first real love, poor true-blue to the core Andrew, dead now like two-thirds of my friends. I kept a pile of stones outside, on the railing. On the worst nights I hurled them, shrieking *Shut up!* at the tree.

———————

Finally I managed to sleep and awakened to knocking, a metallic banging in my hangover armor. The girl's arm was draped on my chest, her legs tucked into mine. I disentangled myself and saw she'd peeled off the jumpsuit. She had on only panties, one shiny black string extending from butt crack to hip, black polyhedron in front, as worn by Hollywood pirates. I staggered across and reached for my bathrobe. When I got to the hall I heard the key in the lock and knew it was Perry. There he stood in the doorway, backlit by blinding October. Raven-haired, apricot-limbed, cheeks and chin formed in heaven.

Hi, David, he said.

Mere inflection made me want to forgive him. Those blacker-than-black eyes, faultless, no hint of duplicity.

I came for my wok, he said. And salad spinner.

I don't have your salad spinner, I said—still adjusting the rope on my bathrobe, cinching it tight. You must have left it with somebody else.

I'd forgive him as always, I imagine he figured. I wouldn't. But then maybe I would. I'd just stump around limbless, all torso, and hit my barnacled rock again and hang on. Pain would be welcome, let him wreak what he might. Just to have him back. Just one last night, a few hours. One little hour. I'd play the doormat, doorstop, doorman, anything. I'd be his groveling fling.

Well, he said. Are you going to make me coffee? He eased down at the table.

I could see by his look I was potential again. Weeks had elapsed, I'd suffered enough, was ripe for the stinging. I shook coffee beans in the grinder, pressed the button, poured water into the maker, spilled. Perry said he saw me last night at Mecca. He'd wanted to talk but I disappeared. I started to say what good would it do, but was interrupted by a thump. A thump from the bedroom.

Perry stared toward the hallway, then looked at me.

Oh, so. You're not alone. Anybody we know?

It's not what you think, I said, almost admiring his acting. No hint of hurt, no jealousy. He had to feel something.

David, he said. You miss me so much you have a man in your room.

He had it half-right. There's no man in my room, I avowed.

The girl appeared in the hall, brushing her hair, clad in my baby blue T-shirt. The coffeepot gurgled.

You must be Perry, she said, pure dauntless composure. I'm Davy's niece.

At first the situation was sitcom—Perry said, I didn't know David had a niece and Gwen said, yawning, eyeing the coffee, Well now you do—I'm from Nevada. *Oh*, Perry said; Gwen said, I'm looking for work, yawned and said, Davy what's for breakfast and opened a cabinet, pulled a box of Lucky Charms down and stuck her arm in. I was astounded. You'd think five hours of sleep had set the clock back eight years. She acted and looked like a bratty high schooler.

You want to have dinner this weekend? Perry asked, a bit later. I'd poured the coffee.

I don't know, I said, sipping—partly for Gwen's benefit, hating to seem the wimp in her eyes.

I'll have to see, I told Perry.

After he left I boiled water for oats, cut a grapefruit in two and presliced the halves, clicked the toast down, arranged bowls and plates, glasses for juice. I buttered the toast and set out jelly and honey. We settled to eat, silent. Birds twittered outside. Steam rose from our bowls.

I see what you mean about him, Gwen said. Poor guy.

Poor guy why? I said.

He's miserable.

He is?

He doesn't know what he wants, she said. He just drags you in, spreading the misery.

I put my spoon down. This hadn't occurred to me. I'd been caught up in my own nightmare, I guess. My own colorful hell.

Really? You think?

I mean, it's not your fault he's an ass. She stuffed a big bite of toast in her mouth. A jet rumbled overhead. He is, she said, chewing. Can't you see that? Look at him. He's miserable. A poor selfish miserable ass. She washed her toast down with juice.

Pretty one, though, she added. God.

I got up in a while and poured more beans in the grinder. I'd called in sick at the store. I *was* sick, though better, I'd had aspirin and water and the coffee was helping. Outside, my flowers still shimmered, or some did: roses, tiger lilies, hydrangea, late bloomers. But not for long, winter was coming. Soon the stalks would stand budless, or leafless, bent sticks asleep or dead in the chill. A pair of birds perched on the birdbath, dipping in, hopping back to the edge. Drops rainbowed up in small haloes. I paused, filling the coffeepot, noticing the state of my breathing, and felt something shifting inside me.

The next day I'd take Gwen and her bags to the Greyhound station, bisecting the derelict districts, past strip joints, rock clubs, peepshows, adult video stores, right past Mecca in fact, its litter-strewn walk, dumpster-bums in the alley, its saggy roof and pale front, like a whore in her robe in broad daylight, no makeup. Gwen would head home, back to green Pennsylvania. She missed the woods, her family, if not the rain. My poor daddy needs me, she'd say.

And me? For a while I wouldn't know. I wavered, there at the window, hating hell but calling it heaven, Ponce de León to a specter, part fable, part lie, there and not there at all. The boy could grow up, miraculously. He could change over time, he could change overnight. I was patient, if not terribly tough.

Gwen snapped the rubber band on the newspaper and spread the pages on the table. I switched the coffee machine on and sat back down. She roved over the comics, legs tucked up on the chair like a child, an eighth-grader, humming, black panty string showing. She looked across, read me a bit, then started to chatter. I fell into the chatter, willing to sit and nod and respond, and waver forever, and do what I knew I'd do when I did.

Poet and Philosopher

The Philosopher and Poet Fail to Put Out the Fire

They stand in the dark watching the cars and carport barn burn. Far below to the left, fire trucks switch up the mountain, all red flash and horn blast and echoey siren. They'll get here too late, the poet is thinking—the eucalypti above the carport will go, then the hillside and cliff and who knows how many homes. Good God, the philosopher thinks: it happens so fast. Inside the structure, where both cars (the philosopher's Nissan, the poet's old Volvo) are swallowed in orange, paint cans and tubs of thinner explode, howling, paint jets flaring straight up. They might have saved the philosopher's car—the poet's poorly wired dash is to blame—but suckled as they were on action-adventure, the ubiquitous four-wheel warheads, well, why get too close?

Look at it go, the philosopher says, flames doing their dance in his glasses.

I'm looking, the poet responds.

A burning board falls from the roof, hits the burning hood of the Volvo. Fire trucks wind up the grade, shrieking.

Why didn't you go for the hose? the philosopher asks. The poet had dashed in for a plant mister, five minutes earlier, and squirted his air vents with that.

Panic, he answers.

Panic, his neighbor repeats.

They've shared the same house for years. Each has his own entrance, own gas and aluminum hearth, and own grand view, deck jutting out at San Gabriel Valley (smog-choked by day, transcendental by night); the poet's carpet's more pretty. The philosopher lives above, his friend on ground level, as Plato deemed it should be. They're employed by the same four-year liberal-arts college, a network of ears and quick tongues, and thus keep all discussions, and actions, top secret. (The poet's erotic machinations, and confessions of such, to be honest, tend to be vivid and awful, with much more potential for ruin.) Humorously, if awkwardly, too, each can hear the other's every sound in the house, down to each sigh, love grunt, and belch. The acoustics astound.

You got that girl in the house? the philosopher asks, turning—meaning the nineteen-year-old student he met (he knew her from school). And couldn't help hearing.

She's in there.

Hiding?

With a groan and great hissing a falling beam slams the Nissan. Sparks leap to the tree branches.

She's afraid they'll make her a witness.

Her father'd kill her if he knew. Right? Not to mention your job.

No answer. The Nissan's windshield explodes.

The philosopher knows. His friend's a philosophical riddle, a mixture of Schopenhauer, Epicurus, and somebody else—Captain Kirk, maybe—but bone-skinny, dark-skinned, prone to teeth-gnashing and worry, with black hair on his shoulders and back. They've confided a lot, the man's a good buddy, if a little unstable—unlike the philosopher, a swimmer, robust, blond, soon to wed his old college flame; his only weakness is booze.

The trucks hit the summit and curve out of sight onto Skyline, veer over to Edgeridge and, whipping dry branches and dust on the roadside, fly down the private drive to the house. Men in glow-in-the-dark extraterrestrial outfits trot up with gargantuan hoses. They spray, knocking cracked glass from windows, sending charred mirrors and grill ornaments flying. Now that it's safe—salvation is nigh—the poet affords himself leisure to feel what he's feeling, what he's felt for ten minutes, to maybe use later in the form of a poem. The philosopher begins to relax, realizing how thirsty he is; visions of beer steins dance in his head. Across the yard, past the rose garden and fountain, the girl peers from the house (inseparable, almost, from the dark).

I've got to clean up, the poet says, half to himself, facing the collapsed blackened hull of his car. This, he says, says it all.

You refer to the girl, the philosopher ventures. Girls, I mean.

No answer.

They gape at the mini-barn's skeleton, stubborn last pockets of flame, the steaming ribs, the jigsaw melt of tin roof. The firemen spray. A paint can does a jig by the Volvo, rolls down the road.

Don't get all symbolic on us now, the philosopher says.

Well look at this. Look at me. I'm not even *insured.*

Mine'll cover mine.

The poet glances across toward the girl. To where the girl must be.

This is it, he announces. I'm cleaning up.

Do it, the philosopher says. Just do your work and eat your brown rice or whatever.

And forget her.

Forget her. The other one too.

I will, the poet declares.

Good, says his friend.

After tonight. One last night. Then that's it.

The blaze is extinguished—the mountain is saved—though the firemen maintain their positions. It looks like it's out but there's heat underneath: flare-ups occur, as both poet and philosopher know. Tonight, later, they'll quaff a whole fifth of tequila and ten bottles of beer, once the girl is gone and each realizes that the other can't sleep. In the meantime they hover, and ponder and notice, now that the steam is diminished, the glowing of stars between rafters.

The Poet Vows

Lying in bed sleepless he vows, starting now, to start rising early and not forsake work, those fertile morning hours. Then again, writing and reading are addictions like anything else; sustained sleep has its place, within reason.

He vows to make peace with his body, limit the fat, sugar, and salt—to eat his brown rice, or whatever. And tell his neighbor no, when he can, to hard liquor. Everybody suffers thinning hair, finally, the slump and iguana eye-pouch. No one accepts, though some suffer more.

He vows, wrenching his damp frame in the dark, to spend cash with less stupid abandon. The new sports car he bought to replace the burned Volvo, a car he'll hate in three months—toy-tiny, you can't see the hills through the miniscule windshield—sank him in debt. (The landlady, by contrast, pocketed ten grand in insurance, opting to Band-Aid the barn: new supports merely, and a fresh tin roof. The philosopher pocketed seven, settling on an older replacement, and was surprised to see the sports car roll up. Your pecker signed that contract, he told his friend.)

To not say or do cruel things to people, or vehicles, or animals.

To find a woman with whom to have things in common. Bonds built on the physical, or worse, the teacher-mentor dynamic, will fail, not to mention, upset and unhinge, leave you the dry salt pile you're asking to be.

To stop misrepresenting. To say you took a walk last night in the graveyard reciting Yeats when in fact you stayed home, waiting for Letterman to come on to have someone to eat with, is a lie, however romantic.

To believe in belief and keep living. To avoid the existential quicksand midmorning, or the office when the sun wanes in the blinds. To not dwell, mind inky with thought, on splendid wrecks that once were the future, but plod on, despite that empty bullet-shell heart.

He vows to neglect any vow, if need be—briefly—for the sake of overall good, of necessary forgivable weakness. For love, however immense and irreparable.

Poet, Philosopher, Dog

Aseat on the porch the philosopher refills the shots, tipping the bottle; the poet cracks a pistachio. The valley swells like a bright circuit board. The smog has dissolved; everything shimmers.

To the dog, the philosopher says—meaning the landlady's dog, which oddly has vanished—raising his shot glass.

To the dog, the poet chimes, raising his.

May it never return, the philosopher adds. And then grimacing, gulps.

As always, it's hot—October's still summer in greater L.A. Both sit in gym shorts and sandals, no shirts. A lit candle squats on the table. The poet's out of sorts because his friend's said he's leaving. The landlady, who lives down the hill, won't hear of a girl, or wife-to-be, moving in, her apartments are Gentlemen Only, so the philosopher must make an adjustment. He's house hunting already, forsaking or about to forsake this fretwork of light, this bastion of purity in the blight that surrounds: drive-by, carjack, kidnap and rape and cop-drama terror, not to mention traffic, the countless crisscrossing freeways. How could he *move?* the poet wonders (underpaid, high on ideals and the view). All paths lead downhill from here. Besides, the poet is jealous. Things cooled, degree by degree, as his friend waxed matrimonial. And now the dog, which they mutually hate, nay, conspire against—that crusty ill-mannered flea-blown hopeless non-creature—has disappeared, too.

How are your balls? the philosopher asks, referring to the poet's recent vasectomy. Not so recent, actually—he's endured the ache for five months.

Ball, he says, touching himself gingerly. The right one. It's still acting up.

You might slack off more.

I did, the poet responds. He cracks a sealed pistachio between his back teeth, then fears for his molar.

Completely?

Mostly.

Give it a chance, the philosopher says.

The world's come apart, as they say, on the poet. Sex hurts, walking hurts, it hurts just to sit. (Okay, he'd gotten the dozen ejaculations out of the way fairly quickly, bent on the sterility check, then unfettered fun: and forgot the part about ice.) His young lady isn't returning his calls, and the other's away, out of state, for a while. And now his one good male friend, his confidant, confessor, is leaving. Granted, he'll inherit the philosopher's quarters, where the view is much better. You can see the burned carport from here, the mountain in winter, miles more of the valley. But who can say how long he'll last himself? The landlady's old, and old people die—once she kicks it her thousand kids'll step in, knives and forks sharpened. And out the poor poet will go.

Three tequila shots later they hear the familiar toenail click on the lower deck, the familiar thrice-circling, slower than usual, the groan and collapse. Poet and philosopher stagger up, the latter snaps on the floodlight. The poet descends to welcome the brute. The philosopher observes from above.

Long weekend, boy? the poet says to the dog.

It's a shepherd-mix mess with a ghastly exterior, the fur missing on the lower back and sides and hind parts, not unlike a baboon. Legions of fleas speckle the gray and pink flesh; the huge charcoal balls are obscene. Worst of all, though, is the odor. You can smell it eight or ten paces off, more if there's a breeze.

The thing lifts its head, blinking, thumps its tail on the deck. Obviously the beast is unwell. It'll come skulking up as a rule, fawning, mewling, pure hangdog—vile proof of the phrase—a nightmare caricature of American Fido, loyal dog pathos, reeking its nose-wrecking stink. This above all else is why poet and philosopher hate it. Not because it's gruesome, putrid, pathetic—it can hardly help the fact that the landlady, still in her own head a Wyoming rancher, won't do a thing to relieve it—but because it *knows* what it is, and works that to advantage, inviting threats and abuse, hangdogging up despite your injunctions, inciting the cruel you that you keep under wraps, the imperial you wielding the broom *(Go! Get away! Go!),* bouncing kindling sticks off the scab-addled hide.

Another toast, the philosopher intones from above, crossing the porch for the bottle.

The dog can barely raise its head. Softening, the poet bends to stroke its snout—something the philosopher won't do—where the smell is least potent. He's both relieved and sorry it's back, he'd rather not ask himself why. He sighs, then climbs the stairs, goes in to wash his fingers in the philosopher's sink.

The next day, the landlady gets news from the neighbors. They returned from Tucson to find, inside their fenced courtyard, her dog clamped to their own, their expensive Dalmatian, swollen, stuck fast—they'd called the vet, evidently, to pry them apart. Chances are, they tell the landlady, they'll have to settle on something. Liability for paternity.

By this time, however, her dog has expired.

Death by overfucking, the philosopher says, a day or two later, in his kitchen.

The poet nods, says nothing.

The philosopher stands at the stove in his baby-aspirin-orange shorts, adjusting the flame on the burner. The poet leans on the counter, hairy-backed, shirtless, sweating, in his usual dark mood. The air conditioner's broken, and they can't open the windows, thanks to the smell. The landlady had her quote-unquote Mexicans bury the dog in the garden, a yard or two off, unbelievably, from her tomatoes and string beans and squash. The coyotes dug it up promptly by moonlight, disemboweled it, tore at its flanks, so she's reinterred it herself, cursing, but didn't get it quite covered. The mound outside is rank, a patch of stiff fur visible still, riffled by wind.

The philosopher drops pork strips in the wok, which hiss as they hit the hot oil. A pot of rice steams on the back burner. Stacks of boxes stand all around—he's half-packed, he'll be out in a week, snug at home in the house he's found by the college, a nice place, roomy, old, with no view. In a bag by the door are leftover cartons of flea-bomb, bequeathed to the poet (the old tenants left the door open often, the dog had crept in, and though the philosopher'd set off two dozen bombs, eggs were still hatching).

The poet guzzles his beer. He can still smell the carcass—sweet, horrific, huge—through the closed window, the walls, the tar-shingle roof. The philosopher dumps the remaining pork in the pan. The poet sees himself supine on the table at his HMO doctor's, straining up on elbows, in pain, eyeballing tubing and tissue, strangely his and not his, pale hamburger meat.

We're glad it's dead, the philosopher says, stirring the vegetables in. That's what it comes down to.

That's it, says the poet, not altogether sure he agrees.

The problem, you see, the philosopher says—waxing philosophical—is that exulting in the death of things living calls into question our basic humanity. Indeed, he says, pushing his glasses back on his nose, this is the question. It's dead, it was born to be dead. And we're glad. That's hard to handle.

They take the plates and forks to the table, open fresh beers and dig in, still batting paradox around, moral and existential conundrums. The philosopher flexes his mind. The poet embellishes, taking mental note, storehousing tidbits to work up later in verse. They eat, talk with their mouths full. The poet takes a second helping, forgets to blow, burns the roof of his mouth. The philosopher's logic escapes him at times—he doesn't traffic in such, in some ways distrusts it. But his friend's in rare form. It's good to eat, drink, and spout off.

May the dog rot in peace, the philosopher says, beer upraised.

In pieces! cries the poet, one of his giggling fits coming on.
May the coyotes strew him all the way to El Monte—
May his rotten limbs flap! Unburied! Unwept!

The gloom's gone for a change. The poet forgets his girl's tossed him off, stops fearing the notion that he, unlike his friend, may not be (or be fit to be) married. Of course they'll keep meeting, he thinks, here and in town, new wife or not, though his guts say it's unlikely. The new tenant will be quiet and pleasant, he's certain—he can't imagine at this point the brash young man who'll move in, stereo blaring, the unending shouting (*Fuck, dude, fuck you!*) He even stops feeling bad for the dog. And expels that lingering thought: I could've bathed and cared for the beast, which, given health and affection, would have survived. No, like the hotelkeeper told Inspector Clouseau, it wasn't his dog.

Lights twinkle on in the valley. Dusk settles. The gloom's gone completely. The poet's all overflowing spontaneous feeling, so welcome in this time of no time for tranquility. He loves this man, he decides. His good true friend and fellow fire-sufferer, the philosopher. So solid and cogent, so much more upright, forthright and free of deception, than he. He'd like to say as much but can't, afraid he might cry. He imagines them mashing the dog underground thirty years hence, by letter, whatever, wherever they are, united in death by what they hated alive. All the more poignant, it seems, for on some level, with dinner over, the brandy bottle out on the table, he knows it's the end.

Later, downstairs, asleep and in bed, clad in jockstrap to protect the raw plumbing, the poet dreams of the ultimate girl, a mishmash of girls he's known and many he hasn't, the exactly right girl, who must, who does, who simply has to exist.

Asleep also, the philosopher—too philosophical to be the Christian he was as a child—dreams of heaven's tribunal. He sees the dog on high at the right hand of God, flaring its ethereal nostrils. Penitent, shambling up to the throne, the philosopher kneels, the radiant father rumbling above: *Pet the dog! Pet the dog!*

The Dead Know Too Much

At Zephyr, as elsewhere, the dead transmit from their graves. As elsewhere, the stones are fitted with video feeds, and mourners with cordless headsets receive postmortem tidings, recorded premortem, of course, and timed for release via the internet at appropriate intervals. One will witness, inset on a stone (in closeup, the face deeply shadowed, retouched somewhat), the deceased lending comfort, if not placating, or softly making amends. There'll be verbal sweetmeats for dear ones, suggestions, instructions, life stories, jokes. There'll be final word, to the degree that the dead can and should be believed, on estate, that ugly ongoing suit. There'll be reasons for living and dying, if not celebration, if not promise or hope.

At Zephyr you won't find wandering criers—they who will, for a fee, bewail your departed loved one, no matter how long ago passed. Nor will you see synthetic willows, nor oaks a la Savannah, dripping the pale plastic moss; there is no bridge of sighs here that actually sighs. Mourners are asked not to bring picnics, or (as elsewhere) to jog between stones, or do Tai Chi or yoga, or the sit-ups and leg lifts in black Lycra. At Zephyr, poised on this cliff facing sprawling Lake Simcoe, foaming and freezing in turn, mourners mourn with tact and respect, headsets or not.

Take Harriet Sibbald-Tuppage, for instance. One sees her here often, fixed on a marble bench in the fenced Sibbald plot, dating from 1780. She'll unlatch the ancient gate in the ancient fence and slowly take her seat, slip on her headset, click the code on the transceiver, and hear the latest from her late husband Harvey. He seems to have plenty to say; one wonders where and how he found time to record so much before his aneurism whisked him away. Since she is a Sibbald, the top rung of families, and owns the best resort on this stretch of coast (boasting lakefront cottages, an endless sculpted golf course, shimmering swimming pools, spas and massage, canoes and kayaks, badminton, squash, and croquet), she isn't concerned about money. She was first to convert to laser mode, costly and rare. Since mid-April, Harvey's appeared in 3-D, projected several feet out from his grave, a grinning hologram—large as life, as they say—if not the whole of him, half, anyway, whatever the camera caught, a broad bald bust with an elbow, a small section of forearm; or at times just the head itself, suspended head-high, bobbing periodically for emphasis.

On windy summer days like today, she'll have her dark purple windbreaker on and gray warm-up pants, a scarf maybe, and the contempo black and gray shoes, which look like something somebody might wear to go bowling. Today she's here very early—in and gone, she'd like to hope, before the gawkers and oddballs arrive, the necro-gothics and weirdos and winos, your idle leering carbound Yank, morbidly curious, amazed to be on foreign turf without boarding a plane. It's dawn, or just past. Here Harriet is on her bench, fenced in, headphoned. Harvey appears in the mist. Half of him, anyway.

As usual, he offers the tender tidbits. He calls her his honey pot, his Pookie, asks how his peach blossom is. He's sorry he's been silent so long. It's been a week; he's transmitted every three or four days these eighteen months since he died. He offers the usual tips about business, exquisitely timed. There are annuities to consider, securities, commodities, futures. There'll be new shares to purchase, and sales and trade-ins. She'll need to ride the accountant, crack her whip; she'll need to closely oversee what he's done.

She's got her pad out and pen at this point—she takes cryptic notes. The lake smacks the shingles on the lakeshore below. She hasn't been exactly well herself these days. She was on her way out, she thought, a month or so after Harvey; she spent seven strange weeks in the hospital. But she recovered. Her lungs rose again on their own, her head cleared, and in time she felt good. Reasonably good. Today she feels odd, edgy and shaky. At least she's functioning.

Harvey pauses, as if allowing her time to jot everything down.

What about bullion? she murmurs. Gold futures?

Harvey's head looms larger. His shoulders and neck disappear.

Forget metals, he says. Market's too bullish, I think.

Once again her skin crawls a little. This isn't the first time he's anticipated her question, or questions. Yes, they always did think and speak from one mind—but lately it's all seeming too weird, and too much. The market wasn't bullish in the least when Harvey died, nor when he taped these epistles. Nobody'd foreseen the turns the economy took these last months, and there was no way Harvey could either. Nor could he have known who the present prime minister would be, which he apparently did, hinting as he did at the antics of this nitwit Paul Martin. And the pointed recent smut Harvey'd alluded to, occurring now in the province—well, it frightened her. It made her feel crazy, or set up, messed with, abused.

Pookie, he says, his head says, afloat in the mist.

She clicks her pen shut, melting, suspicious as she's feeling. And then sees a shape by the fence beyond her great-grandmother's grave. She plucks the transceiver up, pauses the tape. The transmission.

What, she calls out.

The person stands unmoving, indistinct, leaden. The fog's thickened; the wind has picked up. Waves batter the beach.

Who is it? Harriet calls.

No one, the person replies, gliding cautiously nearer beside the steel fence. He materializes, at least partly.

He's short, slightly plump, clad in a respectable suit, not showy. The woeful expression and droop in his shoulders imply he's a crier. Criers aren't forbidden outright at Zephyr. They're hired, now and then, on formal occasions, aiding in easing the floodgates of grief. But solicitations are never, never permitted.

I don't need any tears, thanks, Harriet says.

The man stands slumped at the fence, clutching his black hat at his abdomen.

I know, he says.

Elm branches creak, to the left. The wind whips in hard. The crier sighs, if crier he is.

She does miss her husband, needless to say. They met when she was freshly divorced, or almost; they slogged through that mess as a team, carefully, tenderly, and things got better, and then incredibly good, and stayed good, despite Harvey's occasional arrogance, his penchant for sneaking sex in public (with her) and for unceasing talk. He'd fix her eggs and toast and tea each morning, he'd pack her lunch, and prepare thoughtful dinners, a creative if not award-winning cook. He didn't work. He didn't have to; he just managed her money and planned long lazy trips for them, intricate tours of outlandish countries: Iceland, New Zealand, Finland, Egypt, Nepal.

She shifts on her bench, forcing more air into her lungs. She tightens her scarf. The man stands there, unmoving.

What then? she asks.

The dead know too much, he says.

She sits listening to the wind and the lake and elm branches, taking this in.

About what?

Everything, the man says.

Harvey appears again suddenly, or Harvey's head does, unbidden. Harriet tries to pause the transmission; she taps the remote.

It doesn't respond. Harvey continues, as if impatient to finish. His head floats between her and the stranger, the crier, if crier he is. The scalp shines so brightly it glows; the blue eyes seem impossibly blue.

Honey, Harvey's projected head says. Don't forget the garbage goes out on Sunday.

We can't stop them, the man says, looking stricken.

Sweetest sweetness, Harvey says.

What do you mean? Harriet asks.

A jogger puffs past in the mist, skirting the row of stones by the cliff. He's got reflectors on his wrists, his Adidas.

I mean we've set them free, the man answers.

Harvey's head bobs. It's nice here, Pook, he says. You'll like it.

She's standing at the gravestone now, a fat granite slab flecked lightly with mica. She prods a button beside the monitor.

It's a scam, she says. The computer knows him so well it does him better than he did.

Maybe, the man says.

We pay to see the deception. It's fun. I want to believe it. But it's a scam.

Sweet Pookie, says Harvey.

Zephyr, a voice calls from the speaker.

Turn him off, Harriet says.

Who? the voice asks.

My husband. Stop him.

There's nothing here from Mr. Tuppage, says the voice, which may or may not be a robot's.

The man at the fence is weeping suddenly, quietly, covering his face with his hands.

I'm here for you, Peach, Harvey says.

Nothing new from Mr. Tuppage for a month, the voice says. We're not transmitting.

The man's weeping grows more distinct, more distraught.

Harvey, stop, Harriet says, addressing the bobbing head.

We're the same, Harvey says. You and me. The same dust from the same dead comets. The same light and heat.

The stranger wipes his nose with his handkerchief, saying something Harriet can't decipher. He takes a step back. And then disappears in the mist, as if he too were transmitted and abruptly cut off.

Do you need help? the voice from the monitor calls.

The monitor flickers. Then the following message appears:

Zephyr denies outright any deception or falsehood, any ghostly trickery, any and all tampering with video feeds. The dead are dead, clearly. Mourners are expected individually to safeguard their wits.

The mist thickens. The wind rattles the elms. The lake roars, blasting the rocks and the cliff. The head no longer floats over the damp grass. Harriet turns to retrieve her remote. She's not well at all, suddenly. For a moment her lungs seem to surrender, to fail to fill fully. And then there Harvey is, projected a yard off or more, in full, crown to brown loafers, sitting, beaming, leaning back slightly. On her bench. He's wearing his apron. The gray kitchen apron.

Are you there? the voice says.

Harvey's patting the bench now, saying Harriet, hey, I made dinner.

She backs up a step, totters, then rights herself. She can't seem to get air in her lungs. A truck rumbles west on the highway, en route to Port Bolster, or Painswick, or Sutton. Her husband beckons. A gull wings silently in.

Record Shop Girl

I am a musician of sorts, but the fact is I'm lazy. I might have played anywhere and with whomever I chose, but didn't, and don't. Instead I tune up and play for myself; I play solo at home. I go to concerts for pleasure and listen to albums. I sit in the chic spots on Melrose and Sunset, jotting my musings down on a pad, then type them up later to send out as reviews. I slouch at the compact tableclothed tables here by the windows, watching as women march by like notes on the sidewalk, short-haired women in tights and glossy black leather, long-haired women in paper-thin skirts, hair glowing every shade of red in the scale—I sit here at Josef's, or at the Eton or Onyx, sipping iced coffee in the roar of the city while women flow through my face in the glass, my once-younger-but-still-acceptable-face, which is also the face of my sister, my sister who's gone.

After coffee I do the record shop grind. I haunt the places I've haunted since before I was born, seeking and buying on streets my mother once shopped. I save the big store on Highland for last. It does the sort of volume I need and require, replete with its share of odd used surprises, the trickle-in recordings I assume have vanished forever. It is my kind of store. And then there's the girl at the counter.

Today I linger at the D's and the E's—Debussy, Dvorak, Edgar—disinterested, bored as a cat, waiting to see if she's noticed. She has.

Right on time, she says when I get up to the counter. As usual, she's wearing her smile, a smile for which most men would cleave off their hands.

Oh yes, I say in return. I ease my gems onto the counter: Shostakovich's Fifth—an early Berlin Philharmonic; some unheard-of old Purcell and Ives; a few other less notable items.

I didn't see these, she exclaims. She waves her wand over the spines of the albums, dissolving the spell that trips the alarms. The glare of the overhead lights reflects in her glasses, which have a vague pinkish tint. I'd have saved these for you, she says, if I'd known.

You have to work hard, dear, to keep up with me.

Her smile grows even more sprightly. Hers is a face that enchants. I work fairly hard, mister, she says. Harder than you, I'd guess.

Her colleague, the kid with the Clorox-bleached hair, whisks off the people behind me, scowling as always, and starts ringing them up. He thinks I'm invading his orchard—that I've already shaken the branches and tasted the fruit. He's wrong, but I'm not letting on. Indeed, he's got a right to feel jealous; if I cared more about things in this world I'd be jealous of *him*.

She slides my records into a bag. She's got this unearthly ethereal calm, she's part Chinese or something, dark-haired and tall, and her wit seems aligned with her beauty. A rarity in men and women alike.

Well, Barbara, my friend, I say. I take my bag by the handle; I'm not so hot on goodbyes.

Well, she answers.

The woman that the kid has been helping is scoping me out.

Her eyes veer away from my butt, from this girlish thirty-inch waist I adhere to, in spite of my years. Mostly it's these Italian pants I'm wearing; I buy them for this. I look young. Too young for the way I've been feeling.

I know what Barbara is thinking. I've still got your number, I tell her. We were considering a concert, weren't we?

That's what you said. You said you got tickets for nothing.

Clorox glares over again. I tell Barbara I'll call her, and to keep an eye out in the meantime for stuff I might need. I thank her, give her a kind of nod or a bow, and stroll past the sensors with my bag in my hand, past the blinking white columns, out into the sunlight.

I proceed on the circuit. I drive back to Sunset to pick up my shirts, do the grocery and bakery, then head up the hill to where my mother is housed. The Home is an elegant old-fashioned Spanish affair, only the finest: stucco walls and polished tile hallways, plants hanging in pots, all the earthly delights and conveniences. A button my mother can push at her bedside, if she thinks she's in trouble. Her lovely antique piano, which she won't play any more. The stereo I furnished myself; I threw out her old one and wired the new, hung the speakers on high.

The narrow parking lot is full. I circle the block until someone steps up to a car, wait, then back slowly into the slot. I turn off the engine and pull out my key. The air conditioner hums into silence. I'm parked on the crest of the hill, hood leveled at the grinding heart of the city. Sunset is an hour away, but already the sky's full of the apocalyptic oranges and pinks that make newcomers gape, wondering if they're alive or dead. Below, on a lesser hill, a blackened tar-trailer is puffing up smoke. Rows of palms flank the street, dead still in the tremulous air. I try to find energy to get out of the car.

My mother was a famous concert pianist. She grew up in New York and moved out with my dad, a man I can't remember at all, a conductor-composer killed in Korea, blown to pieces by some new

Chinese bomb. My mother knew Glen Gould and Furtwängler and others; she performed with the symphony here in its earliest heyday. I don't blame her for not playing now. If my hands looked as twisted and gnarled as hers, I'd wear mittens most of the time.

My mother pushed me hard. She pushed me in grade school, pushed me in high school and college, she pushed and pushed, saying I'd be better and brighter than any, which might have been true. I could have done with my bow what my father'd begun with his baton and with fresh ink on score sheets. I could've done what my sister would do with her keyboard, had she continued. My sister was the purest, most natural among us, and did not resist the motherly pushing. Her swelling arpeggios would make you sit down and weep, anyone would, even the layman, even this poor dolt down there raking his asphalt. I still have her on tape, a tape I keep in the drawer with the photos. A frozen heaven of sound, the sound of my twin at eighteen, two years before she left us and married, and—I hear—gave up the piano.

My mother we disappointed to tragic proportion. It's no wonder she's fallen apart. But I couldn't do what she asked, not after my sister had gone. I settled for the smaller ensembles instead—this during my stint at the conservatory, and just after. And then that was it.

I've still got my keys in my hand. If I don't get out of the car now I won't do it at all. I check my face in the mirror. The white sack from the bakery sits on the passenger seat—a few of the chocolate chip muffins she likes. The road-patching men are all packed, wiping their foreheads and climbing into the truck. It's gotten hot in the car but I don't dare open the window, not with the smog, this vibrating lurid pink twilight, which makes street signs and roofs seem to quiver. In the sky to the south only Venus appears; at this hour it's all that breaks through the gauze.

My eyes trace the grain in the solid wood dashboard. I chose this machine for its leather and teak. For the quaint wooden bar in the back, which I've never used. I haven't touched the tape deck either. You can't listen for real while you're rumbling and bouncing along, it's an impure experience. You might as well listen to Chopin or Schubert on skates, careening around assaulting your ears with a Walkman.

That's it. I'm not going in now. She'll last another couple of days. I see her every week. Every two weeks, at least.

I push the key in and turn it. My engine roars into being. Tepid air blasts out at the vents. I'm feeling hungry again. I need to get back to reviews, I'm so far behind. I've been even more lazy than usual. I pull out on the street and coast down the hill. Street lights are flickering on. To the left, the skyline towers up in the murk, a huge fuzzy-lit Stonehenge, an outer space vision.

They say Rossini only cried twice in his life. The first time he cried because his mother had died. Later he wept while picnicking with friends in a boat on a lake when a whole plate of chicken breasts fell over the side. Breasts stuffed with delicate truffles, which Rossini loved to no end and called the Mozart of mushrooms.

I've never loved, I'm afraid, or even liked things with passion — so in this sense I'm completely unlike him. I'll never be a drunk or a glutton, or any kind of addictive what-have-you, since I am mainly indifferent to things, be they people or spirits or food. I could've been the new Jascha Heifetz, but it's not in me to feel what he feels. To know the passions that matter, which I get only in glimpses and patches, heat-sparks that come with the cracking of ice. I play for myself. I sit in a chair in a room full of records, solo, playing for me, my playing as strong as when I was twenty. I play what I think I have lost, led by the sheer weight of memory — for this sister who inhabits my dreams, who lurks in mirrors at odd moments, in gaps between chords, and in the face of the record shop girl, this living ghost of the city.

The record room is full to capacity. Records range from ceiling to floor on each of the walls, with barely an inch of available space. To be truthful, some are my mother's, they're mixed in with mine, fine old recordings from the forties and fifties. Day by day they're increasing in value, all of them, like these baseball cards collected by morons. In the next room is a full wall of tapes and another of CDs. Along with boxes and boxes of disks I still haven't opened, the ones they hope I'll review.

I'm slow at reviewing. I'm dull and tired much of the time, lazy as sin. Lately when I do mail a review off they send it right back, saying it's no longer relevant. They tell me to tone down my language. They don't care to hear about incontrovertible timing, or melody's disarming flow. Transubstantial sevenths and fifths.

I pad into the living room, fresh-showered, wearing my towel. I put on Satie and sink down on the couch. I pull on the headphones. I cross my legs on the coffee table, pushing the magazines to one side.

We taught ourselves timing, my sister and I. We learned more than anyone might have imagined, rehearsing night after night, surreal duets, our harmonies mingling, reverberating the soft quiet peace of the house. We slept in the same bed until high school, and after. It was a hard habit to break. Each night she'd slip into my room and crawl in beside me; now and then I'd slip off to hers. We'd embrace until daylight, until the calamity of traffic flared in the distance and the wailing began. We'd lay under that cool white cover of sheet, jigsawed together, one single calm being, our breathing metered and measured, lungs falling and rising in effortless tandem.

Mornings, my hands grazed the plump new swellings of flesh on her chest—there was no question of warrant or license, no sense of shameful impurity. My hands traveled her pale long belly, down to the curling dark hairs, which seemed to increase overnight. Sometimes she'd touch me in kind, though not so forthrightly perhaps. We'd lay locked until dawn, until Mother got up to make coffee. We'd lay there entwined, my stiff still-miniature self nestled in the cleft of her buttocks, awakening to beauty, the unfiltered grace of the soul.

I take off the headphones and get up from the sofa. Satie roams in the room, willfully idle. I step across to the window. Miraculously the haze seems always to lift in the evening, leaving a night-scape so clear at times it's sublime, a strange lovely gridwork of twinkling, shimmering light, a jewel-studded sorcerer's cape flung on the hills.

I suppose it is possible to make oneself cry. But that's cheating, I think. One could always seek out criers as models, famous un-happy weepers in books. Jake Barnes, say. Or that blubbering slob in Saul Bellow, seizing his grief at a stranger's funeral in steaming New York. It's not like I don't know how I am. I did not choose to become cynical. I didn't set out to turn bitter as this, to dismiss this city and world as completely as my sister dismissed me, my mother and me, running off with her unmusical petroleum engineer of a husband, telling me to leave her alone.

I have of course little cause to complain. I don't have to work. My house is paid for in full; I bought it after Mother sold the old house in Westwood and went to the Home and made me the official cosigner. I tend to spend a bit of her money. I tell her I do, and I tell her what for. I couldn't begin to put a dent in her fortune, with compounding interest and all.

I ease into the chair by the window. I pick up the phone. I go over the sequence I've arranged in my head, combining clauses and verbs in fair orchestration, then dial. The tones sing out as I press with my finger. Barbara picks up at her end of the line.

I drop the phone in its cradle. She's not supposed to be home. Either she's gotten off early, or she's sick, or she's adjusted her schedule—I thought surely I'd get her machine. I'm ready now to ask her to the concert, but the living voice is a kink in the chain link, a hampering unthought-of dimension. My lungs deflate. I feel flushed. The background roar in my head rises up, like tape hiss, or waves in the distance.

My history of interactions with women is a history of failure. A sad fact of my life. But this woman is different, and this is the point. She's devoted to listening and playing. In our chats at the store she has taught me a bit, a bit about contempo classical and jazz, even punk and new wave, about which I'm poorly informed. She's sharp and intense and assured, dark-eyed and lithe, and seems to invite my advances.

The moon's floating up in the east, orange as a pumpkin, preternaturally bright. I face the window, gazing past my reflection. Satie hovers, rhapsodic, dreamy.

I intend to give her a chance to withdraw. To come up with excuses. I won't put people on the spot. She can call *me* to respond and say yes, fully assenting and eager. I can comply with willing compliance. I'll call again in the morning. I'll be sure then to get her machine.

Under even minimal pressure, it's the one-man performance for me. The toccata, the solo recital. The syncopations of everyday human transmission are strangely beyond me, they're messy. I prefer probes over capsules, prefer the triumphs of the Voyagers and Vikings, and of the unmanned Magellan, streaking along even now toward its business on Venus—prefer them all to those early Apollos, or this flawed and disastrous shuttle, to bodies strewn piecemeal over the desert of ocean.

—————

And so it happens: we go to dinner, Barbara and I, and to the concert. To Luigi's on Western, to Brahms and Tchaikovsky at the Chandler Pavilion. I entertain her with a tour of the record room and the parlor and deck and show her my violin collection. I share a little tale about the death of Tchaikovsky, a terrible death, unjust and unnecessary; he died from drinking bad water, they say, water tainted by cholera, water that should have been boiled, but had not.

Then we sit in the living room drinking white wine.

This is some house, she says.

Thank you, I answer.

I fill her glass up and then top off my own; I'm taking it easy. She's wearing her black and white tights, the ones with the dizzying horizontal patterns of stripes. Her black leather jacket hangs on the chair by the door. In the dimness her face seems less Asian than usual, her chin-line and cheeks a little less rounded, her nose, below the rims of her glasses, the nose of a very young girl.

This is some wine, she says, smiling her smile. And looks at me.

Are you okay? she says.

Very okay.

She rises in her tights to reinspect the piano. She uncovers the keyboard, tucking the cover carefully back in its tray. She runs a finger over the long row of ivory. Delicately—so soft the keys don't make a sound.

Jesus, she says.

Pretty, isn't it.

Pretty isn't how I'd put it.

Put it however you like.

She pulls out the bench and sits down. May I play?

I'd be honored, I tell her. She leafs through the music on the holder, then stands and takes down a sheet from above: Sibelius, *Concerto for Violin and Orchestra,* piano reduction. She flattens it out on top of the others.

You're one for the cool arctic strain, I say. I know you like Grieg.

I'm for anything sounding as lovely as this, she replies, and plays the opening bars.

She's not bound for greatness, exactly. Still, she's learned her lessons and has at least a feel for the movement, which is more than you can say for five-eighths of the musical world. She's played this piece maybe four hundred times and it shows, she knows it inside and out. Now she simply needs a good teacher.

I move up to the bench and sit beside her. I turn the page when she's ready. She warms into the song. The playing turns fluid, her pale fingers supple as cream. She gets better and better. I glance at the mirror on the wall to my right.

We could be my sister and I, side by side like this on the perch, dark-haired, she turned in profile, the same height as always as me, and me still solicitous, still boyish as ever in some ways, though careworn and slightly more shaggy.

She stops playing abruptly.

Are we going to break out the violin, or what?

I look at her, then away.

That's what you want?

Of course, she says, smiling, her eyes on the score sheet. Why else would I choose this one, Mr. Record Collector?

I start to get up, hesitating. I don't know about this. I stay where I am, then on impulse gingerly pull off her pink-tinted glasses. I put my mouth over hers. The timing is right all at once. The stirring is there.

My, my, she says, drawing away. She sets her hands in her lap, straightens her shoulders.

I go out and come back with my best violin. She starts the song again from the beginning. I haven't played with a soul in ten or twelve years. Soon I am hating myself for hating the way she fails to draw out the rests, for how she sometimes drags the rhythm. It's not fair to hate somebody for this. To imagine your senile arthritis-bent mother doing it better, much less your beloved lookalike sister, who should be by now the best in the world. Comparisons are odious. They're downright unfair.

I sail away on the solos regardless. I seal up my eyelids—I don't dare glance in the mirror. I'm working from memory and do not leave out a note, not even in the final movement, where the notes stream out like bullets, or debris on a fast-moving river. I think she approves. We play three or four songs. We finish the wine and open another bottle, then we're down on the carpet, her shirt up to her neck, arpeggios of laughter trilling from her lips. I explore her, bold from the music and wine. I kiss her body all over.

You play a mean fiddle, she says, before I get very far.

Drifting from the speakers is Shostakovich's Fifth. I fall into the waves of strings, inching up again to her chin, pausing, meandering, no hurry at all. She's not about to resist.

Eyes closed, I see my old bedroom in Westwood. My first violin standing there in its case. I hear piano-song wafting up from downstairs, that haunting lingering melody I've been hearing for years and can't seem to escape, that requiem for the living, and loss of one's hope. I've kept away from women for ages. Except when I pursue them to tease them, which is mainly teasing myself.

Barbara pulls me onto her body. She's strong. She unbuttons my pants.

I'd forgotten what it was like. This kind of wonder I'd all but erased from my mind. I fall in completely, I don't know where I am. The impromptu folds me under its wing, begging for nocturnes of unrehearsed feeling. Eventually I hear her calling me back.

What? she's asking me now. What are you saying?

It's not the first time this has happened, the dark *sotto voce* augmenting until it gets me in trouble.

What do you mean?

You keep saying Unfair, she says, out of breath. Unfair, it's unfair, you keep saying.

You must have misheard.

Distrust washes over her face, or vague disappointment.

I guess so, she says. And slowly draws her hips into mine.

All at once I'm churning with hatred again. I can't help it. And then my mind misgives me for real. I know from experience that the show is over. I may as well pack up my instrument now, toss in the towel. Learn to throw off the tyranny of womanly charm, I've been swearing for years, certain that the project was hopeless. Lately, with these variable hormones, my body's taken the swearing for truth, dull as my thought-heavy brain.

She tilts us onto our sides, working herself out of her tights, which are bunched at her ankles. It's okay, she says. She brings her lips to my forehead.

Of course it's okay. Okay for her. She can fly off to her shop and have fun with her workmates. She can talk about me if she likes, about how rusty I am with my bow or whatever else, things over which I have precious little control. She can stand at her counter discussing the latest new-wave-synth-pop or post-punk band—bands about which I know or care not a jot—and she'll know what she's saying. She's a dozen years younger than me, easily. She's only a step or two up from these teenaged goth-rockers, baleful dark bunnies driven by irony and their scorn for the world.

Only memory's sublime. Surely I'm better off by myself. I don't even know what to say to her now.

Gradually her breathing lengthens and deepens. She's drunker than I am and she's falling asleep. I'm drifting in and out of slumber myself, hips tucked into hers on the carpet. I float with the sound floating down from the speakers, the lamenting mournful violas and cellos, the cadenced footfalls of snare drums, which rap like jackboots on concrete. Louder and louder it gets, the horns growing more nightmarishly brash, the drums more insistent—which is impossible, I set the volume myself.

There is little to fear. My body's fine, my mind is intact. I know how to dress, how to behave. I'm at the helm here. Lazy or not, control is the key, so what if I'd like now more than ever to cry and it's not in me to do it. It's a matter of mind. Of arranging perspective, of hearing and seeing precisely, of timing. If need be, you can even fasten fruit back onto branches, freeze it together again, even after it's fallen, or shattered and bruised. Even with half of you missing and the rest of you scattered over the railing, sinking, fading by degree into water, cold and unwhole.

Good Is All You Know
How to Be

A good week for business, but not fun. The car show this weekend wiped out supplies, root beer and chocolate for shakes and long
Coney buns. Another girl quit; Buddy's lost three girls this month.
And now Karen, his wife, has begun to suspect—about Buddy,
about Laura Lee—saying if he doesn't start to act like he's married,
well, he soon won't be. So Buddy's been good. Unbelievably good.
He got through this week, and today's Sunday rush, without caving in.

It's time to clear out but the cars keep coming, gurgling up to
the speakers to order. There's a '58 Chevy Yeoman wagon, bright
copper, fully restored. A '53 Ford, club coupe, turquoise on white,
sun spangling off its projectile bumper and grill. Buddy peers from
the kitchen, filling frosty mugs at the antique Coke fountain. It's
hard to the squash the nostalgia, the blood, sweat, and gears, the
lucid daydream these people seem to be living. Where else should a
vintage car go for a meal but a vintage drive-in? Timing's the issue,

is all. He's wiped out, his back aches, he's low on French fries. He can't be paying more overtime.

Laura Lee scoots up with an empty tray. Ponytail, candy apple red lipstick, saddle shoes. She's his age, almost—mid-early-late forties—but looks younger. Much younger. Her pinstriped gray apron is stained.

Serve or shove off? she asks.

Serve, Buddy says. But that's it.

Outside, she hooks an overfull tray on a pickup—Betty Boop BL&T, chili-cheese fries, a pair of State Fair corn dogs, Buddy's killer steakburger, chrome canister malts. Buddy stands at the window, prodding the kink in his back with his thumb. A bus passes out front; the gargantuan maple, blindingly green in full leaf, looks blurry in the damp heat. Thirty miles north is the lake, that monster of moisture, of wind chill and lake effect snow after the good weather's gone. Laura Lee glides to the sidewalk. She flips the hinged painted-wood sign inside out and positions it to disrupt the entrance. Instead of Caution: Curb Girl Crossing, the sign now reads BUDDY IS CLOSED.

The last of the in-store diners file out, crying Bye, Buddy! Buddy snags the plastic baskets and wax paper, wipes the last table and chrome table jukebox, and dusts the neon Elvis. He straightens the model cars in the windowsills. The flatbed Ford and Buick roadster, the white and red Chrysler carryall, the '39 Woody. The bubble-eyed 1950 Dodge pickup, pine green, little chrome ram on its hood, just like the truck he learned to drive on as a kid. Hank the cook scrapes the grill, Jill his helper mops. Laura Lee divides the tips between the girls, Sarah and Vernell and Sue. Buddy does want this weekend, this month, to be over, for sure. But when today's over, when this workday is done—when Buddy and Laura Lee are left here alone—Buddy will have to say no. Will have to tell Laura Lee no. He's vowed, promised himself. No whim wham, no beer binges, drugs. He has sworn on his life to be good.

He's always lived with lies, right. But lately the life doesn't suit. His wife's talking divorce, he can't sleep, his back hurts; even his dog Nipper seems to be nursing some grievance. He hears his own voice at work and thinks it sounds forced. Un-Buddy-like, fake. He's bored with his spiel, the rap that, well, makes this place BUDDY'S. You know, these little cars here are where people go who don't tip. You want to stay stuck on my windowsill, Pablo? Spend the rest of eternity inside a Woody?

The girls skitter off one by one in their polka-dot sundresses. Hank and Jill yell their farewells; they slam the backdoor. It's just Buddy and Laura Lee now in the lobby, Laura Lee counting coins out at the till.

Jesus, Buddy says, I'm about wrecked.

She doesn't look up. Thirty-eight, thirty-nine, forty, she murmurs, clinking. She jots figures down in the book.

She controls incoming and outgoing funds, does payroll; she runs the place, more or less. In the year she's been here she's revamped the bookkeeping—and rescued his business, basically. She studied business at the CC, and knows what's what, unlike Buddy, who enlisted right out of high school, and worked tool and die twelve years. He learned business the hard way, mistake after mistake, spending every last cent his dad left when he died. Buddy's tossed great gobs of money away. On overpriced meat, on antiques, on new asphalt, on faux period clothes for his girls. On Caribbean cruises with Karen; on flying lessons. On rare scotch and cocaine. Especially cocaine.

He steps into the mop closet for cleaner, a damp rag. His black and white floor tile is scuffed.

Buddy's dad, Buddy senior, was the fifties guy, actually; Buddy was raised in the sixties and seventies. Karen's been deriving a kind of bizarre pleasure pointing this out—at least until lately, when new suppositions started eating her up. Buddy's at the drive-in too much, she insists. And she tells him why. It's a chrome-plated monument, basically. It's morbid, she says. It's father worship. Your dad's dead.

It's history. It's memory, Buddy will sigh.

It's a tomb, she insists.

Good haul today? Buddy grunts, glancing at Laura Lee. He's bent over now, scrubbing.

Laura Lee slips the stacked bills into the money bag, zips the bag shut.

Good enough.

Good enough's better than not enough.

Good enough's good enough, she says.

Behind her on the wall is the thrift shop mirror Buddy'd embossed in hot pink: Do Not Exceed Recommended Dose of Nostalgia. In the nook to the left are the antique Coke bottles, Crush cream soda and Fanta and Nehi and Squirt, and assorted citations and ribbons, and yes, the framed family photos: shots of his dad, mainly. Dad with this or that of his hot rods. Dad with the bird dogs and guns. Dad on the boat coming back from Korea, docked in the mist in the murky Pacific; Dad at the mic onstage with his bad boy proto-rock band. This was a man who knew what he liked and took what he wanted and was loved by all, especially by Buddy, who he sometimes ignored. This was a man who boozed and bedazzled and crooned, and went out without fuss—head first, in fact, off a Triumph tri-chopper, into the hood of a speeding dump truck.

Laura Lee snaps the ledger book closed, heads into the kitchen.

She looks as good as the high schoolers he hires, trim and smooth as she was thirty-one summers before at Camp Cavinell, where they swam in the lake and rode horseback, burned marshmallows, endured lessons in Jesus and snuck off to the woods to neck. Camp Kill Yourself, they called it. Tiny, she was, with eyes as black as her hair, which cascaded miraculously down to her butt. Yes, he was her first, and she his. But at that age who can restrict himself to one girl? He strutted and sampled and stepped on hearts, the way young people do. Then the sampling ended: off he went to the military, and came back to find Laura Lee married; and then he too was hitched, with a baby boy and girl in the bargain. Laura Lee at least hadn't had kids. No little psyches to wreck when she split with her husband.

On the island counter in the kitchen, Laura Lee's unfolding a crescent of glossy paper over a fake '50s platter. Buddy stares, dropping the damp rag in the laundry. She scrapes a good bit of the white onto the plate with a paring knife and starts chopping.

I know you don't want any of this.

He turns the faucet on at the sink and rinses his hands.

Laura Lee, this isn't fair.

She keeps chopping. She divides the little hill into rows.

What isn't fair?

This.

She plucks a plastic straw from the box on the shelf and, undoing the wrapper, cuts it in half with Hank's knife. And then bending down, slips the straw in her nose and snuffs a line up. And then another.

Buddy dries his fingers. He hangs the towel back on the hook.

Since when do we score our own schnoof?

Since the boss said he quit.

He looks at her. At the platter.

Shit, he says.

You didn't run twelve miles today in a boiling parking lot, Buddy. Talk about wrecked.

She squeezes her nostrils together, releases, sniffs hard, tips her head back. The paper packet is open still on the counter. It glistens, a shiny blue and black flower, its white heart a frozen heaven of pollen.

We'll hire another girl, Buddy says.

Two girls, you mean.

Two girls, I mean.

You can take one of them out Sundays after work. Since Karen seems to know about me.

Slow, take it slow, he tells himself. He feels the air labor in, labor out of his lungs. Laura Lee's been saying it might be best if she quit. He can't have that. He likes having her here. She's efficient. Intelligent. Witty. And she hasn't yet taught him her system, this magic she uses to keep him out of the red.

Laura Lee, please, he says. We've been through this.

You've been through it. I'm in it.

A yellow T-Bird noses into the lot, pulsing up past the row of steel posts, each topped with a speaker. The driver's not young; his thinning hair is pomaded back, drawn to a sort of hopeful ducktail. Laura Lee pulls a menu from the holder beside her and gingerly covers the platter.

Buddy can't have her quitting. But he can't have the other, either. Even if she is the best lover he knows; has ever known.

The T-Bird edges up to the kitchen—expecting a drive-through, or something. Buddy wags his finger, shaking his head. The T-Bird moves on.

I don't mind a Sunday drive now and then, he says. Long as we don't—

Stop and park by the lake. I know.

Buddy sighs.

I get it, she says, sliding the menu aside. You made that clear. She wets her finger and runs it over the platter. She lifts the finger again to her lips, runs it over her gums. And adds: Who's asking you to drive anywhere?

Buddy stares out the window, trembling just slightly. His forsythias rise in a jagged line just past the asphalt. They've grown an inch a day since they were planted in early spring. In a month they'll blot out the last present-day eyesore: Napa Auto Parts, the next lot over. And beyond that, butt-ugly Denny's.

Where'd this come from? he says, turning.

Where'd what come from?

He eyes the platter. Henry?

You don't know him.

Don't tell me you're hanging with Henry.

I am not hanging with Henry. You dork.

He's a fat slob.

She dips in again with the knife, scrapes more powder off the paper.

You're not exactly skinny yourself, Buddy.

You're too good for that.

For what? she says, chopping.

He's considered leaving Karen, of course—even-keeled colorless Karen with her crosswords and cakes and Wednesday night church meetings; he could, and knows that his kids, Molly and Buddy the third, would survive. It's just that—well, Laura Lee's not an entirely plausible alternative. She's as defiant and fiery as she is physically lovely, with a temper like a full-grown baboon's. She's got a taste for illicit chemicals, which contributes to his ongoing delinquency. He loves what she stands for, and the fact that she's loved him for years. And she hasn't aged. But she could rip him to pieces, he feels. She could knock his head right off his torso. Which accounts for some of the madness in bed.

Too good for what? she repeats.

The chopping is loud, all but impossibly so. The crunch crunch crunch on the plate vibrates his neck, the base of his spine.

Too good to be with somebody I don't have to sneak with? she says. Too good to give myself half a chance? To give a slaphappy fuck about me?

Maybe I should sample some of this, Laura Lee.

She stands fixed, gazing down.

No, Buddy.

Just to see what you got.

No, no, no.

Cut that other one in two for me. That's all I'll do.

Forget it.

I'm the boss.

This is harassment, she says.

Before long the whole gram is gone and they're down on a clean pile of towels on the tiles by the grill. It's been two weeks, and Buddy's missed this. Has needed this, has been dying for this; he's ready now to die every hour for more. For pine smoke and pine pitch, for humid lake breeze, and these endless black eyes, more madness, more Laura Lee. But things all at once have turned strange. Maybe the schnoof didn't set well with the pill he took at noon for his back. Or maybe this stuff really isn't Henry's, like Laura Lee said. It could be cut with something weird, untoward, evil. Buddy, she warned, save some, we can't do that much.

Whatever it is, Buddy leaves. Floats off, checks out, right there on the towels, in the act.

At first he can't see where he is.

And then he does.

He's in the chair by the bed up the road at the rest home, nodding with Grandmam. She's been gone now a decade but is still droning and droning, unhinged and brittle, a twig snapped in the wind.

He's in the Iowa woods with his dad, shotgun propped at Dad's shoulder—the thundercrack blast, the squirrel tipping from its skyscraper branch, the descent and delicate impact—and Buddy just five, if that, in Dad's woods.

Then he's on the road in the old bubble-eyed Dodge, beloved pickup, tuning the radio in. Laura Lee's beside him, leg pressed against his, gripping the quart of Pabst in its brown paper bag; he hasn't had his license for long. The radio whines, it crackles and pops. Then it's his own voice rasping through the dash, spilling the trivia: America's first drive-in, The Pig Stand, acclaimed for pork sandwiches, sausage, popped up in Texas. Roller skates all over were rare—most lots were gravel. Eckard's in Canton outfitted its carhops as clowns.

And now Laura Lee's at the wheel, and it's Little Feat on the radio, and then The Dead. Buddy cups her nearest breast in his hand. He buries his nose in her hair, nuzzles her neck. She calls him Sugar Pumpkin, Apricot, Button, names he's forgotten she used. Where are they heading? Where else? Back to Camp Cavinell, the pine trails and soggy mold-smelly tents, lake waves gently lapping the shattered gray shingles.

They fly past the last outpost. The toy town, toy buildings—post office, butcher shop, five-and-dime, the pharmacy/soda—replicas all, light plastic, pastel yellow and blue, poised to collapse at the first hint of wind. Laura Lee flings the beer bottle and bag out the window and hits the gas hard. She's upset now about something, that much is clear. He's been good so far, the cheating came later, it can't be that. For now good is all he knows how to be.

Sweetie, what? he says, sitting up straight in the seat.

They roar past the camp entrance, the weathered cherrywood sign and replica ramshackle booth, the featureless plastic attendant. Laura Lee picks up more speed, pushing far past anything any engine like this one in any toy truck might handle. The tiny ram on the hood is glowing bright orange. Smoke pours from the floorboards.

Stay with me! she yells over the roar.

Baby, I'm yours, Buddy yells.

And he is. He's been on this joyride, in Dad's rattletrap pickup, forever, fixed in this long humid smoky July. He loves her. He's with her. And will be. Forever. The dead end and cliff lay ahead, the great gray lake evanescent beyond, white-capped, breeze-teased to texture, like frosting, like faith or fidelity, like asphalt, like memory.

The Painter's Wife

It started with a circle of pebbles. He noticed it one evening driving up. A kind of pea gravel Stonehenge, there on the concrete walk by the shed. A tiny note was tucked under one pebble—he unfolded and read it as his car ticked on the gravel drive. Beside the walk his daffodils bloomed, outrageously yellow, though it was mid-winter still; tonight the snow would resume and that would be it, they'd die standing up, exposed like the mirage this warm weather was. Penciled on the note was a phone number and a woman's first name, one he couldn't place despite the tiny message penciled beside it, and he still wouldn't know till he called, five frozen days later, and she said, I'm in the painting hanging over your bed (I have been watching you sleep, the note said). So he invited her over, the painter's wife, the note writer, pebble layer, and they drank chardonnay, studiously avoiding the subject of spouses, until at least she explained why she came, though it never sounded right, and he couldn't say what she wanted, even if she did do what she said she would do if he didn't mind, and sat by herself on the bed in the bedroom and stared at the painting, at her face in the paint, re-claiming whatever might be living or left, as she said, to reclaim.

She sat on the bed with her notebook and pen and drank down her wine, then joined him in the kitchen and he poured more, and they sat on the carpet in front of the fire and talked about spring, about summer, and off came her sweater, her bare shoulders sculpted and smooth, tanned in that impossible midwinter way; they wound up in bed by the painting, under the wan pleasant face that was hers, if less recognizably so (she was happier then, slightly fuller), and she stayed but stole away very early; and they carried on after, after that night, but not for long; she seemed untethered, too precariously sane, prone to non sequiturs and unintelligible e-mails, and she'd slip out of bed in the dark before dawn to do God only knew what, whatever she pleased, wander the house in the nude, he didn't know.

But when she drew near he could tell, he'd feel her gaze and slowly open his eyes, or open one eye, and there she'd be by the bed, standing in dim silhouette, rigid, unmoving, and he'd feel afraid, as well as confused, not knowing why she was up or what she was doing, not knowing if she was staring, and if so, if she was staring at herself or at him, or if she had an ice pick in her hand, or a new note and new stones, or a gun. Needless to say, he got a bit guarded; then he got more and more guarded, and she took the hint and left him alone, she didn't come by or call, and then, well, she moved, all the way back to the town she grew up in, far, far away from her husband, the painter, and him. She worked in a nursery out there, he heard later on, a hot house that thrived year round, come freeze or white heat—and then he heard she disappeared altogether: nobody ever saw her again. Meanwhile he muddled on as before, breaking ice from the gutters, weed whacking, raking, mostly unchanged, unsettled in ways he couldn't name. The pebble circle reappeared with the thaw, altered of course, looking decidedly lopsided, skewed. She dropped into his dreams periodically, pleadingly. The painting hung silent, hoarding its clues.

Somebody Decent

It's trash day, late April. Town's in the throes of spring cleaning. Wrecked sofas range at curbside, flanked by battered dinettes, spent loveseats, toilets, sinks, disabled strollers, playpens, rusty bicycle frames, and box after box after bag overflowing with clothing, bedding, plumbing, mouse-eaten electrical tape, snap-handled axes, brooms worn to the nubbins, and of course the more common refuse—cat litter, dog hair and dirt, the shrub-trim and grass-rot from yards. They check it out street by street, snailing along. Others do likewise, some halting outright, upsetting traffic. The boldest veer off and load what they need in broad daylight. Ed, less bold, if vaguely proud, makes Curtis wait until nightfall; or twilight at least.

He swings left on Ravine, revving his Escort. They cross Cherry, Cranberry, Peach. Buds have opened on trees, unfurling over the rubbish. Bluebirds yammer in branches. The sunset's begun, beyond the outlines of factories, the smokestacks, and creek. There's a lamp he could use, orange-pink, no lampshade. This ruined end table, ahead, could be glued and clamped into shape. Thanks to the bonfire he made, weeks ago, behind his apartment—he'd burned everything ever having to do with his "intended," Irene—he's been lacking. His place is bare except for the TV and stereo and a dead potted ficus. The foam mattress he sleeps on is deranging his back.

You sitting on the floor to eat still? Curtis asks, flicking his cigarette out the window. He's got his black and gold Steelers cap on, the ubiquitous work shirt, black boots.

I got a pillow now, Ed answers. Fat thick one, like you hippies used.

Curtis tugs at his beard, briefly. He wasn't a hippie, really, but takes the comment in stride.

I'm into furnishings, he says.

Curtis and Ed worked the same line at Tri-Co for months, assembling neoprene door panels for Ford. Curtis had seemed impervious to Ed's flinty terseness. Ed was lulled by the calm, somehow, that paunchy Curtis emitted. Curtis found work elsewhere, finally, first at a tool and die, then at a foundry, while Ed lingered at Tri-Co, where he was promoted to manager. Good thing you left, Ed said, a while ago at the Deerhead; they meet there now only rarely —Curtis has a wife and a kid to support—to drink and throw darts. The guys on the shift hated him now, Ed said. They called him Butt Cheese, said his bunghole sucked wind. They did the Deerhead again lately and Ed spilled his guts over shots of Wild Turkey. He had to tell somebody, he'd've gone crazy. Irene had just said, That's it, she'd had it with his meanness and moods and his overwaxed piece of shit Escort. Fine, go, Ed had replied. And she did, tossing her engagement ring on the carpet. What about this stuff we bought? Ed yelled, indicating the furniture. Irene didn't answer, just stamped down the steps. Ed phoned and phoned, quaffed the rest of his vodka, drove by Irene's place and her friend's and her dad's, drove by again, then gave up and sped home and snapped.

He flung the vodka bottle against the radiator, stomped up and down, bellowed, kicked a hole in the wall, and, limping and sobbing a little, flushed the ring down the john. Then he yanked the sliding door open and began hurling stuff out. The bed first, brand-new headboard and all. Then the dresser and desk and night tables, the dining set, the sofa and amber stuffed chair and footrest, the coffee table and bookcase; even Reeny's great-grandmother's mahogany rocker, regrettably. He tossed out the photos, mementos, all the love notes and cards, along with her food in the cupboard, the no-salt chips and diet crackers and such. He dragged every last item to the fire pit, splashed gas over it all, struck a match, and, his rage reaching its crest—he knew by now what he intended was brash—touched the match to the fabric.

I'd a paid you good cash for that, Curtis said at the Deerhead, numbly appalled.

Up the hill past the college, traffic has eddied. A pickup's pulled over, or half-assedly tried. A woman's finger points from the passenger window, assessing. Scrounge, Ed grunts, gunning around. Curtis gapes at the junk stacks as they pass. A box spring and mattress loom against a tall maple. Crates spill over with broken tiles, empty paint cans, tar paper, shingles. A tricycle, sans seat and front wheel, crowns the bright heap.

What we need is a truck, Curtis says.

What *you* need is a truck, Ed says, turning.

Curtis has his tobacco pouch and papers out—he's rolling a cigarette on his belly. Ed brakes to let a pair of college girls cross, motioning, eyeballing the butts as they pass. His engine sputters, hacks a few moments, dies. He turns the thing over again, cursing, revs it in neutral, then pops the clutch, burns rubber. Curtis doesn't look up.

I could use a bed, Ed says, a block or so later.

Curtis licks the seam on his cigarette paper, nodding, twisting the ends. The fading sun shines in his beard.

Really, I mean, Ed says, prodding his lumbar.

Curtis nods, striking his lighter.

What Ed wants to say is Curtis, what's the report, as in what's Irene up to, what is she thinking. Curtis's wife's sister works with

Irene at a daycare in Custard. For weeks the wife's sister has let news leak circuitously, not willing to speak directly to Ed and thus hamper her friendship. Needless to say Irene's not talking to him, she hasn't for weeks. She threatened to get a court order, to "restrain" him if he called or came by again. The problem is his friend's wife is no genius and his friend's memory is iffy. Ed gets the feeling that the report is defective, lacking accuracy, like these sentences you'd whisper as a kid, kid to kid, in a circle, just to warp meaning. Curtis told Ed a while ago, for instance, that his wife said her sister'd said Irene said Ed was a dildo, an immature dildo, and that he'd never grow up. Irene of course is Catholic, still half hung up on Jesus, and would never say "dildo." She might have said "dodo" . . . but "dildo"? She was about as likely to use that word as use the implement in question. Irene was reported to imply her dad had abused her—wrong, wrong!—and that life with Ed was, or would be, more of the same. So intense was it lately for her, too, she'd been learning to masturbate: this last, Ed assumed, a perversion of "meditate," something she did from time to time mention. Ed, she said, is a hothead, to paraphrase the chain-voice translation. A walking volcano. A short guy with six dozen chips on his shoulder. So caught up, so frantic, he doesn't know squat anymore.

Leave me alone, Reeny had said.

Ed had called her at work again at the daycare; it was the last thing she told him before she quote-unquote cut the connection.

I mean it, she said. Bug me again, we won't even be *friends*. Do you hear?

The wedding had been set for late June, now less than eight weeks away. Ed's still grinding his teeth about that. The calendar taunts him. Likewise the clock. Spring itself is a taunt, since it ushers in summer. Furniture and beds are flies in his ointment, as are household appliances, pets, attractive women, children, bowling, shopping, drives in the country, TV, and food. He's sick to the guts, frankly, pretend to himself as much as he likes that he isn't. What else can he do? Not rise up off his foam rubber pad in the morning, not hot-shower the pain from his lumbar, forgo breakfast again, forsake his job? His job is all he has now, that and his empty apartment, which he vacuums and sweeps twice a week, need it or not. His dad died when he, Ed junior, was three. He doesn't get along with his mother, who resettled years ago anyway in Florida. Even his fat uncle and cousins left for Kentucky.

———————

Dusk drops. They cruise north on Hemlock. The homes and lawns are expansive, the trees venerable, well-pruned. Almost nobody lounges on porches, Ed notes. He veers left at Clover. Garbage is sparse; people here seem to have less to offer.

Guy'd have to get the thing dry cleaned, I guess, Ed says, spying another mattress.

Get what cleaned?

The bed. Dickhead.

Curtis blows smoke out his nostrils, eyeballing the sidewalk. You want the report?

You got one?

Yep.

Spill it.

Eat shit, says Curtis.

Between Keller and Houser Ed finally pulls over. They inspect a set of mag wheels, a collapsed china cabinet, boxes of socks and undies, baby attire, soiled tablecloths, placemats, Harlequin romances, broken bricks, plastic beach buckets, Easter baskets, a gigantic stuffed rabbit. They hop back in the Escort, move up the block and climb out again, inspecting, sifting. Before long the trunk and backseat are brimming, every last item chosen and loaded by Curtis. Ed can't seem to find anything he likes. If he opts for a mattress they'll have to use rope, i.e., go fetch it and cruise back and lash the affair to his car. He could just carry on bedless, of course. Say, Fuck it, let his back go to hell. Cripple himself. Use up all his sick pay and disability. He could stay home a whole year in his bathrobe, just drink and beat off and watch the shit-eating soaps.

Curtis's driveway is cracked and grease-stained. The grass, or

rather weeds, in his yard could stand trimming. The carport, yon-
der, is so crammed with junk he can't pull his ailing VW in, come
rain or come snow.

Reeny's dad's got a flatbed, Ed says as they pull in to unload. He
yanks on the emergency brake, killing his engine. Curtis's young
daughter appears at a window, drapes flanking her Down Syndrome
face.

Curtis looks over. A birdcage rests in his lap, bent badly, rusted
around the rim at the base. He looks confused.

A truck, Ed says. Two-ton.

Curtis puts one and one together. Oh, he says, peering into the
cage.

They unload and take off again, pausing at choice spots on the
way. Ed has to bungee his trunk shut at last to fit everything in. They
pull into the drive-in beer distributor on Dill Street to pick up a
case, a cold one. Then head west, and north slightly, toward Highway 198 and beyond, where Reeny's dad lives. The asphalt is littered
with roadkill. Possums, coons, groundhogs, and skunks. With his
one headlight Ed can't see as well as he might. Once or twice he fails
to swerve properly, soiling his freshly-scrubbed tires, whitewalls,
adding insult, as the phrase goes, to injury.

So what's the report? he says finally, over the harangue of his
engine.

Curtis gapes, as if Ed's just spoken Bulgarian. He tips his
beer—they've got sixteen-ounce talls in their laps.

The report is there ain't a report, he says, swallowing.

Ed's been by a few times to see Curtis in his yard sale setting,
where Curtis unloads what he's scraped up at yard sales before,
items priced at a dollar or a quarter or fifty cents more than he
originally paid; where he sells, in season, whatever he scavenged on
trash day. They'll sit in beach chairs in the drive drinking strong
coffee, shock black, the kind Curtis likes, while passersby trickle
in, Curtis's angelic harebrained young daughter clutching his pant
leg, Curtis absently petting her head. There'll be ancient mow-
ers, snowblowers, "furnishings," clothes racks, and ten or twelve

card tables laden with knickknacks, plates, cups, toys, tools, fishing reels, old pistols, clocks, a power cord snaking out from the house to plug in the razors, radios, blenders, and Mixmasters to prove they do indeed work. Curtis isn't awfully quick on the draw, but he's decent enough, despite the all-out flat-on-his-face drunks that Ed, more often than not, helps him begin. He's got a kind of muddled nobility, a stoutness of spirit. Even if on the worst nights he pukes on himself, maybe soils your upholstery.

Chubby Cindy, the wife, keeps inside as a rule, her nose in her astrology book. She doesn't like Ed, obviously, contributing as he does to her husband's delinquency. She never saw a guy, she told Curtis at one point, with his houses so shadowed by Mars.

———————

In Hicknell, the gas station is closed, as is the butcher shop, and Sav-Rite, and hardware, and combination suntanning-video store. The buildings need paint. The hail-damaged roofs are unsightly, haphazardly patched. People dawdle in yards on lawn chairs under the white-purple bug-zappers, on screen porches, or in portable screen-tent gazebos. Nymphettes skitter about in their summer dresses, all tautness and shining hair. Ed can't help but stare, half-sick, awash in rebuke.

He'd met Irene six years ago at a dance here at the volunteer firemen's hall. She was born here, schooled here, churched here, here with her loudmouth widower father—who Ed likes, actually, and vice versa—and some four or five beagles, all trained to sniff down raccoons. It turns out Irene's dad had hunted with Ed's dad, eons ago, back when the big bucks existed, which made Ed okay, even if he wasn't Catholic, or a particularly church-going type. Pete didn't seem to mind, either, that Ed was thirteen years older than Reeny. Skinny baby-faced Ed looked young for his age. The kid could hold onto a job, and had benefits, and a retirement plan. So what if he didn't hunt?

Ed had been planning to visit, sort of. He'd called Pete after the breakup to find out how much he knew. Pete said stop over anytime for a beer and a snort, they could watch a hockey game, or anything, thanks to his fabulous satellite dish. Ed could say something to Pete tonight that would get back to Irene. Something helpful, maybe. Something to let Reeny know he was sorry; that he was trying, or wanted to try. With a bed to load and Curtis's coffers to fill, they'd have reason to scoot away early. Pete could accommodate overmuch if deep in his cups.

Pete's turn-of-the-century two-story house looks better than many. His shrubs are trimmed quaintly. His lawn, even by street-light, looks greener than green. Ed and Curtis rattle past up the block. Pete's new Buick gleams in the drive, the great white flatbed looming beside. Ed pulls a U and floats back, coasts up to the curb. He and Curtis get out and crunch across the red gravel toward the lit porch. The beagles start in behind the house, hacking and howl-ing, rasping their frantic choking-hound sounds. Before Ed can knock the door opens. It's not Pete, but Irene.

Reeny, Ed gasps, feeling culpable, like the bona fide stalker he must seem to be.

Her black hair looks longer now, blacker and fuller, trailing over her shoulder. She's got a shimmery green dress on, one Ed doesn't recognize. Mascara on her eyebrows, subtle. Lavender eye shadow. She's on her way out, evidently.

What do you want?

Reeny, Ed stutters. I—we—

I told you leave me alone. Do I have to call the police?

We came to see Pete, Ed says.

Pete's truck, says Curtis, his voice full of beer.

Shut the fuck up, Ed says.

You shut up, Irene tells Ed.

Curtis backs off the porch.

Reeny, Ed says, wilting again.

Don't Reeny me. I told you six dozen times. I've had it. Will you listen?

The beagles are hacking it up out back, harrumphing and gagging. Irene's house-sitting, no doubt, feeding the mutts—Pete must be in Canada, hunting. Somehow, subconsciously, Ed must have entertained this possibility. A moth zings up to the porch light, smacks the bulb, then circles madly, upsetting gnats.

Where you going? Ed asks.

Out, sighs Irene.

Who with?

Ed, don't be a dildo. Get out of here. Now. Go.

Come on, Curtis tells Ed. Fuck the truck.

Irene, Ed pleads.

I'm calling the cops, she yells through the door.

They wind up in a bar on 198, Curtis and Ed. It's a fairly new place serving overpriced food—skylights, mod woodwork, pseudo upscale-yuppie, the farthest thing from the Deerhead Ed can imagine. Irene would land here, he knows, sooner than at any shitkicker dump in the township. He parks at the far end of the lot, down where it's dim. He chugs a beer, mangles the can, then stumps in with Curtis to a back booth, fake leather skirted by veined mirror and cedar, where they can see who comes in the door. He's sure now Irene's seeing someone; this'll prove it. In fact, he's suspected it all along. Sadly. Suspicion's what started this, what sparked the fire in the first place.

There's a band onstage in one corner, Cousin somebody, this prissy shaved-head dude of a singer out front with six or eight earrings, alongside a chick bass player, shaved also, in leather pants and blue headband, looking like she'd cut to pieces the first guy who glanced at her sideways. They take turns returning to the Escort to drink, Curtis and Ed—the beer here's way too expensive—one hanging behind to keep an eye on the table and door. The band grows louder, more imperious, fierce, the singer mincing and shrieking. Each bass note jangles Ed's spine, adding fresh pain to pain. He tears a napkin to pieces, sticks the napkin-bits in his ears to preserve his already-poor hearing. Curtis lights a cigarette, assessing the furnishings. Young men in bare sidewall haircuts strut by, designer-jeaned, insultingly bright in their double-knit shirts. The women—some indescribably nice—look to be models, or aerobicized hometown makeovers at least.

At last the band takes a break. Curtis shuffles in from outside, bareheaded, cap flung god only knows where, a tequila belch on his lips. He's got a plastic pint flask in his pocket; something to give the beer, as he says, *ooomph*. He mutters, scratching his ribcage. Then plops down facing Ed in the booth.

She won't show, Ed says, jaw clenched. He's so worked up now he could knock somebody's teeth out. Anyone's. His own.

Curtis shrugs. Didn't think so, he hiccups.

Who asked you to think, fuckface?

Curtis gapes at his beer bottle as if it were responsible for this inscrutable outrage.

You okay here? the waitress inquires, leaning across, ultra-high fashion, tray on one arm—meaning, How long will you sit there nursing one drink? Ed waves her away.

He understands he's been taxing his friend. If he knew how to apologize, now'd be the time. Time to say something to try to salvage this. He feels himself soften, almost. He glances at Curtis. The man's expression is strange. He looks both washed out and flushed, comatose, kindled, his eyes going liquid.

Curtis tugs his beard, sighing. Then speaks.

The report is you're an asshole.

The band's moving into place again one by one under the blue and white lights, drummer first. Every naked inch of his arms is overlaid with tattoos.

She'd a gave you a chance, Curtis continues, if you weren't such a fuck. But you're a mean motherfuck. You ain't human.

Thanks, Ed says, sinking. Thinking: you can walk home, dork.

It's too late, says Curtis. He's on a roll—it's like his planets and houses have lined up for the first time in three lifetimes. For her, he says. And for you. Get it? It's like to make it you'd have to be somebody different. Somebody decent. He feels around for his cap, frowning. Dickhead, he says.

He rises, swaying, and hiccups. He's on the verge of some major pronouncement. His mouth opens, his beard shudders. Then his eyes roll and he turns, upsetting the table and bottles, drops down to scoot out and then vomits, defiling the cherrywood table, spattering Ed.

Later Ed heads down Skeltontown Road, the long back way to town. The car's so full of junk he can barely see out his rear window. It reeks of moldy paperback books, coupled with puke; he did all he could in the bathroom, cold water and borax, to redeem himself for the ride. Curtis passed out when they got to the car. He sleeps now, head aslant on the headrest, inaudibly snoring. You sure know how to pick 'em, Irene might say. I picked you, Ed would reply. He flips his high beams on, rolling into a curve at a saner clip than usual. He signals, veers east on Eden Hill Road. The trunk clatters, straining against its bungee-cord fastening. They pass darkened barns, hayfields, the silhouette of a tractor. Ed feels himself breathe. It's the first time he's felt half-real in weeks.

Ahead on the pavement, a tiny light glows. A fading flare, it looks like, but pale, white-orange, the wrong color. Ed brakes and idles up, window down, revving to keep his engine alive.

A groundhog, legs splayed—roadkill that somebody's squirted briquette oil on and lit with a match. Ed's seen numerous late night high schooler stunts but never has he witnessed this thing. He clicks on his emergency flashers, turns his key off, gets out.

The creature's swollen with rot and heat, supine, its scorched skin puffed up like a wine gourd. Its front paws are clenched in tight little fists, as if in victory, or pugnacious display. Intestinal gas ignites, as they say—and here at the guts a mini-jet of blue flame appears, uncanny, as if the tarrying soul were still taking leave. Ed kneels awhile, transfixed. His flashers flash on the concrete. The wind hisses. The animal sizzles, its eyes boil away. He's tempted to wake Curtis up, share this strangeness with him. But Curtis is zonked, there with his wicker bath shelf and books and dank tarps, his plastic azaleas and sprung swivel desk lamp, his snore blotted out by crickets and peepers, the flutter of corn on the breeze. A lampshade's slid onto the headrest, a little wide white one, lending him the look of a Chinese in a movie, though bearded. With his babyfat beer-bloat and gaping maw he resembles his daughter; there's that hint of Mongolian, an extraterrestrial calm.

Ed should rise and drive home but he doesn't. There's a thing to be learned here, however obscure. The report is he sucks. He doesn't know squat, as Irene told Connie told Cindy told Curtis told Ed. Poor mean motherfucker Ed junior, up to his eyeballs in shit, and not simply sunk now, beaten and blind, but grudgingly seeing—oh, it isn't easy. He could cry now, he thinks, if he let go a little. The frogs and crickets continue their whirring. Cornstalks whisper and murmur. A fingernail moon floats up in the east. The flame falters, dwindles. The animal's fists seem to clench tighter, its strange belly swells.

ACKNOWLEDGMENTS

Unending thanks to Barry Spacks, whose help and encouragement made this work what it is, and made me the writer I am. Thanks, too, to Paul Raymond Martin for his sharp eye and ear, and for his friendship, an ongoing blessing to me.

The following stories appeared, occasionally in slightly different forms, in the following publications: *Another Chicago Magazine* ("Good Is All You Know How to Be"); *Apalachee Review* ("The Dead Know Too Much"); *Gettysburg Review* ("Be with Somebody"); *Kenyon Review* ("The Painter's Wife"); *Paris Review* ("Poet and Philosopher"); *St. Anne's Review* ("Somebody Decent"); *The Sun* ("Still Life with Candles and Spanish Guitar"); *Sycamore Review* ("Salvage"); *Tampa Review* ("Paradise Road" and "Record Shop Girl").

"Hers" is for John Golden.
"Still Life with Candles and Spanish Guitar" is for Jennifer Brady.
"The Dead Know Too Much" is for Allison.